ABOUT T

Hannah Leak writes ̪ ̪ ̪ ̪ sensitivity. She is the mother of three boys. Rather like her protagonist, Posy, she has lost a son, although in very different circumstances. She writes about a mother's loss with great depth of feeling and by using her own heartfelt experience.

Hannah was born in Gerrards Cross, Buckinghamshire but moved to Jersey with her parents when she was sixteen. She is still living in Jersey with her husband, Nigel. Her two surviving sons and four grandchildren live nearby.

A donation from the sales of this book will go to The Compassionate Friends, a charity for bereaved parents. Their support, literature and advice and the support of other bereaved parents went a long way in helping Hannah survive the loss of Giles.

YOUR BEATING HEART

HANNAH LEAK

This is dedicated to all who I love
You know who you are

The sea, the surf, the Island that you loved
Sitting on White Rock waiting for dolphins,
their shimmering fins darting in the water around the tidal
covered rocks between you and the coast of France.
Beach parties, Bonfires, Beatbox, Bacardi,
Brothers, Barbados and Black dog.

Laughter, a lovable guy 'G', the way you drove me to
distraction in your teenage years, all forgiven long ago
Surfing at Secrets, chasing the tide, island life.
Smiles, oh those smiles, seagulls, skateboards and Spider-
man
Wedding party, happiness for the future all gone now
Love, loss, loneliness, that damned dog of despair nipping
at your heels again.

What a life to take, what a bond to break, I'm always
missing you
P. Diddy singing over and over as we take that walk
from ancient church to newly dug grave, in sunshine of a
sunflower hue.
And the people on the beach
enjoying their lives and continuing as normal.

Sitting on the sea wall, ice cream in sticky hand,
sandcastle soon to be destroyed by that ever moving,
constant presence of the sea; today such a glorious
turquoise blue but tomorrow grey.
The chatter of happy people in the background
while I listen to the last song I ever want to hear.
Life goes on, for them but not for you and how my beating
heart hurts.

Hannah Leak, Jersey, 2009

PROLOGUE

The telephone rang in the hallway downstairs. Posy heard it and groaned. She had a sense of foreboding. The cuckoos had arrived from their long journey across Africa and had been calling all day to notify their arrival. Their calls brought back memories that were painful. She was learning to deal with the situation that life had dealt her but it was still hard, so hard.

'It's probably just another parishioner wanting something, I'll let it ring for a while and if Tim doesn't get it they'll just have to leave a message.'

Tim did pick up the phone however and she could hear his deep voice resonating from the hallway. It was Haydn calling to tell them that he and Chloe were expecting a baby. They had been married just over a year and it was a planned and much longed-for child.

'We wanted to wait until Chloe was 12 weeks pregnant before we said anything as we wanted to be totally sure everything was good with the baby. We've had a scan and it's so amazing. We've seen the little heart beating and it looks good and strong, we have a photo too,' he told Tim. 'We have a due date of 1st December so that's exciting, an early Christmas present,' he laughed.

Tim finished his conversation with his son and relayed the news to Posy who breathed a sigh of relief that the cuckoos had brought good news this time. They were both delighted to hear that they were going to be grandparents. Posy especially felt elated and excited at the forthcoming arrival. Haydn had been given a second chance of life after his illness and now he was producing a new life himself. Although he was genetically Tim's child and Posy was not his birth mother she felt as close to him as if he were her own son.

Posy had lost a child. Her only child. He had died in a motorbike accident and when he had died she didn't think she would be able to continue living. This was before she had met Tim and although Haydn, Tim's son, could never fill the void of her lost child she was incredibly fond of him and they shared a close bond. It was rather a coincidence that the two boys were born within a few weeks of each other.

She imagined what it would be like if her son had lived and gone on to have a family of his own. This could never happen now and the sense of loss was almost too much for her to bear.

The due date for Haydn and Chloe's baby came and went. Another week went by and still no baby. Everyone was on tenterhooks. Chloe had been to see the obstetrician who said there was no problem, the baby was doing fine. First babies sometimes came late. If things went on for too long they would take her in and induce labour but to leave it for now.

'Do you know I think this baby is going to come on 16th December,' said Posy with a sense of premonition coming over her.

'16th December?' queried Tim.

'Yes, you know, my boy's birthday. I just have a feeling.'

That would be rather portentous, thought Tim.

The days came and went and there was still no baby. Posy didn't want to keep phoning them to see if Chloe had gone into labour yet;

that would just be annoying. They would let them know soon enough.

Sure enough on the morning of 16th December at 9 o'clock, as Posy and Tim were sitting having a cup of tea in the kitchen, Tim received a phone call from Haydn's number. They both looked at each other with trepidation. Tim put the phone on loudspeaker and they listened to Haydn's elated voice.

'Hi Dad, I just wanted to let you know that Timothy Joshua has arrived. He was born at 8.20 and he weighs 8 pounds. He's absolutely perfect and so is Chloe. Got to go now, you're the first person I've told.'

Posy looked at Tim and gave a smile of wonder, relief and happiness.

'God works in mysterious ways,' said Tim. God has nothing to do with it, thought Posy.

CHAPTER ONE

It was a still, warm night and the scent of jasmine wafted through the open window from the bush in the garden which was directly below her bedroom window. It had been a beautiful late spring day and Posy had been in her garden all day long, mowing the lawn, putting in the bedding plants she had grown from seed, watering and generally enjoying the peace and tranquillity of her hard labour of love in creating such a peaceful haven.

She could hear the cuckoos still calling to each other from the woods at the end of her garden. They had been busy singing a duet to each other all day with the female bird's rich bubbling chuckle and his responsive familiar 'cuckoo.' She loved to hear them and to her it heralded the end of spring and start of early summer. She wondered what poor, unsuspecting bird's nest the female had laid her eggs in. The host mother bird unknowingly incubating and rearing the invader's young whilst her own offspring are unceremoniously pushed out of the nest. How awful for a mother to lose her cherished young, she thought as she nestled down into her own comfortable nest of a bed.

Josh, her nineteen-year-old son, had been in the garage for most of the day tinkering around with the motorbike of which he was the proud owner. It had been a combined Christmas/birthday present from her. His birthday was 16th December and Posy didn't usually like giving him combined presents. She felt it was always rather unfair for children who were born so close to Christmas but this was rather an expensive one so she felt justified in combining the two on this occasion.

They had gone to the garage together and he had picked out the one he wanted, he had a trial run and he was absolutely in love with the bike the first minute he sat astride it. The owner of the garage was a friend of Posy's so she was pretty certain that he wouldn't sell her a dud. Josh was delighted with his new bike and he loved nothing more in his time off on his gap year than polishing the chrome and tinkering around with the engine.

Throughout the day he had been popping in and out of the garage to update his mother with little snippets that he had found out about how it all worked. Most of this was beyond Posy who had little interest in engines beyond her own car. As long as it started and didn't break down that was enough for her to worry about but she knew that Josh loved mechanics and was fascinated by how things worked. That's why he had decided to do an engineering degree at university where he was going the following September. It had been a long slog for him to get the grades he needed. Posy had worked and saved hard and used the money for extra tuition for him. She didn't want for anything but denied herself luxuries if it meant that Josh could have things that he needed. However, she knew that she could earn more if she went in to agency nursing or worked at the hospital but she enjoyed her job at the care home and to her that was more important than money.

Mother and son were very close and since she'd split from Josh's father, Terry her ex-husband, when Josh was five they had been alone together in the house for most of the time. Things had been good at first with Terry, or Terence P. White (as he liked to call himself in business) for quite a few years but Terry's shambolic business deals had been too much for Posy. He had delusions of grandeur and would regularly go out and return with expensive gifts that she knew they couldn't really afford. One evening he came back with a Chanel handbag for her. It was a brilliant present and she appreciated it, but where had the money come from? She had no idea where he had purchased it and didn't like to ask. He had a Savile Row suit individually tailored for him which she had to admit looked amazing but it was all for show and she knew he just didn't have that sort of cash to splash around. He always bought the most expensive champagne to take to other people's houses and if they went to a restaurant with friends he would make a big show of picking up the bill. This only served to worry Posy, as she knew that he didn't actually have the money and was living hand to mouth, from one deal to the next. She never was sure what he actually did, a bit of this and a bit of that. A 'wheeler dealer' is what her father would have called him or maybe in some people's eyes even a 'wide boy'. Nevertheless, he was a very charming man and this is what Posy fell for and many others too so it seemed.

Posy was more practical with money and living beyond her means was not her forte.

The end of the line for their marriage had been the womanising. The phone would ring and when she went to pick it up there was seemingly no one on the other end. She found him on several occasions in the bathroom talking furtively on his mobile. She didn't want to feel suspicious and thought maybe she was imagining things or almost hoping that she was imagining them. However, she suspected it was a female business acquaintance of Terry's who she knew had been chasing him for a while and after Terry had been away on a business trip one time she found she had contracted a dose of something that she would rather not have and she certainly had not been unfaithful!

Eventually enough was enough and although she still loved him and wanted to keep things together for her young son she knew that she couldn't take any more. All the worry was making her ill and she told him that she'd had enough and wanted to part ways. After him promising and pleading with her that he would change and could he stay she kicked him out and had felt a huge surge of relief. She believed he was now living in

Australia and had two other children presumably with the aforementioned female business acquaintance. Josh had contact with him sporadically but he hadn't met his two half-siblings. Posy thought it was on the back burner though and Josh was planning to go to Oz to meet up with his dad and new family sometime in the not too distant future. She was hoping that Terry might offer to stump up the cost of the air fare but doubted it as he hadn't helped financially with anything else for Josh. However, she felt, hope springs eternal!

Posy had been on quite a few dates over the years and had been in a relationship for several years with one chap but this hadn't worked out as he had started to become possessive and was beginning to take over their lives thinking mistakenly that he could tell her and Josh what to do. He was angling at moving in with them and Josh wasn't happy about it and Posy wasn't that keen either. 'I've been on my own for too long now and I'm too independent to even think of having another live in partner' she told herself, and after a few months of anguish and indecision she made the choice and told him to 'sling his hook.' He had taken this badly, a crushing of his ego, and of course, it was turned around in his estimation to be all her fault and she would end up a sad, frigid, old woman. On the contrary, however, Posy had plenty of friends, many hobbies and a job that she really enjoyed as a nurse at the care home in the town. She had a fulfilled life and, of course, she had her beautiful boy and her pride and joy of a garden.

'Hi Mum, the bike is looking amazing now,' Josh came into the garden from the garage and she felt a surge of love and pride when she saw him, his lean, muscly physique and his blonde hair glinting in the late afternoon sunshine. He liked to work out and would go to the gym regularly with his friends. They would joke around flexing their muscles and comparing who had the best 'six pack' of their crowd.

'I can't wait to ride the bike tonight. I'm going to go round to Paul's to meet up with some of the other guys.'

'Okay,' she replied, 'I'll get you something to eat before you go.'

Posy had cooked one of her favourite dishes of lightly fried Camargue red rice. It was too early in the year for any of her freshly picked home grown vegetables but she still had plenty in the freezer from last year and she threw in some broad beans that she'd grown and frozen and also some tomatoes from the garden that she'd dried in the oven and preserved in olive oil. She cooked a vegiburger for Josh as another source of protein as he had become a strict vegetarian over the last few months. He was such a sensitive, thoughtful boy and hated the idea of animals suffering or being frightened and in fear with their adrenaline coming to the surface when they knew they were about to be slaughtered. The very thought of eating the flesh of an animal was now abhorrent to him and Posy understood and was gradually giving up meat herself and definitely felt better for it.

They both ate their meal and talked about some of the funny things that had happened in the supermarket where he was working during his gap year. He'd been watching a little old man who was coming in to the shop several times a day buying bits and pieces. Josh would joke with him and everyone thought he was so sweet. One day, Josh noticed on the camera that this lovely old man had been putting several frozen, ready meals into a carrier bag and leaving the shop without paying. Josh, being the kind-hearted soul that he was, thought perhaps it had slipped the gentleman's mind to pay or maybe he had dementia and was becoming forgetful. The next time he came in however, the same thing happened and several items were slipped into his big carrier bag. He had then picked up a packet of sweets and gone and paid for those and chatted to the cashier amicably and lucidly and in a perfectly normal fashion.

Josh had to tell his superiors about this. They contacted the authorities and the general feeling was that the Police would come and quietly have a word with him but not press charges. Well, it turned out that he was very well known for burglary from years and years ago. As for the items he was stealing from the store, he was acting the Good Samaritan and would offer to do the shopping for all his old friends and then drop it off to them refusing to take any money for his services.

Posy and Josh laughed about this story and she looked over to him and could see that he was learning about people, life, and the way the world worked. It wasn't easy being a teenager; she remembered it only too well. It was even harder being a parent and all that entailed.

'That was great mum, thanks so much. I'm just off now but shouldn't think I'll be back too late.'

'Okay darling, ride carefully, won't you?' She immediately thought what a ridiculous thing to say, why do we say that? As if he's going to say 'No mum, I'm going to ride like an idiot aren't I?'

She heard the powerful bike engine revving up and watched through the window as her boy sped off down the lane to see his friends. She smiled and thought about what his future would bring. He'd had a couple of girlfriends but no one serious yet. Still he was only nineteen, he'd left school the previous July and had been working at the supermarket to get funds together before starting a degree in electrical engineering at Cambridge University in September. He'd had a slow start at school but Posy had encouraged him and got him extra tuition and then he had really bucked up his studying, worked hard in his final year of school and achieved excellent grades. He rather liked the idea of going to a prestigious university like Cambridge and was massively looking forward to it. Further than that, he had no ideas what he would do with his degree once he'd gained it but hoped inspiration and fortune would lead him on and he was full of excitement and hope for a bright future.

Posy cleared up the kitchen and went into the lounge to watch some TV for an hour or so. After this she went to bed feeling happily tired and quickly fell asleep after a lovely day.

CHAPTER TWO

Samantha Woburn Smith, née Morgan, first started having health problems around two years after Haydn was born. She'd have palpitations, feel dizzy and couldn't catch her breath. A few times she blacked out. She was reluctant to go to the doctor but the family insisted and she finally made an appointment to see her GP. After he had listened to her heart he was concerned and sent her for an echocardiogram. It was discovered that she had a heart problem that was found to be hereditary. When she looked back on it she remembered that for most of her life her own mother had been very fragile and had died at only 46.

Sam didn't even get to that stage of her life, however, and died one year earlier than her mother had at the young age of 45. Her grandfather had died even earlier at 43 so, on reflection, there was a history of brevity in the life of the Morgan family, but in the absence of medical attention the problem was left undiagnosed and untreated.

When she was first diagnosed the cardiologist advised the young couple not to have any more children and to take their young son to the paediatrician to get him checked out. He seemed so healthy that they were shocked to find he had inherited the heart disease from her. He was born with a congenital heart problem, which the family weren't aware of at the time. He was a beautiful, healthy baby. He could live a normal life but would have to be closely monitored and take it easy with playing sport and doing anything too strenuous. As he got older symptoms started to show and they were advised that he had a high chance of not living to see his 21st birthday. The young boy was very well looked after by the medical team but the only thing that could help him have a fulfilled and longer life would be to have a heart transplant and he had been on the waiting list for several years.

One afternoon Sam's heart had just had enough and failed.

It was strange really that she had heart failure so suddenly, as at her latest check up the cardiologist had thought there was an improvement in her condition, so this attack was quite unexpected. Her agitated husband, Tim, had phoned the emergency services one afternoon saying she was having palpitations and within an hour she had gone, died in the ambulance on the way to the hospital.

'No, no we were just having a quiet afternoon,' Tim had insisted when asked if she had been doing anything vigorous or become stressed. But he knew what had really happened and would feel guilty about it and seek penance from his God for the situation that had happened that sunny April afternoon. He tried to console himself that she had brought the situation upon herself but this didn't give him much solace. The best way to overcome his shock and guilt was to pray for forgiveness and keep working. He told Haydn through tears of anguish and loss that his mother had died. He was just 19 at the time and had recently started at agricultural college.

Tim met his future wife at the school where he was teaching. He was merely 22 and it was his first teaching job and he was very proud to be working at such a prestigious boy's school that regularly was top of the academic league.

This was his start in the profession and he intended to get to the top. He wanted and would be a Headmaster in the future, that was his ambition and nothing would stop him.

He had walked into the school office one day and there she had been, sitting behind the desk. She was beautiful and he had been taken aback by her looks. She had strawberry blonde hair, creamy skin and a small rosebud mouth that always looked as though she was smiling. Then, when she started talking to him there was something special about her, she seemed to have an almost ethereal quality and he just fell for her instantly and knew at that moment she would be a perfect life companion for him and he wanted to marry her.

He had previously only been involved with one girl and that had produced a few furtive attempts at intimacy, but something told him that he should wait for marriage before giving himself entirely. He had thought about taking up holy orders but in the Anglican faith and for this he was grateful. He knew that he couldn't live like a monk, he could never be that self denying. He wanted a wife, children, to play his favourite sport of rugby, to teach, to help others and to serve his God. He wanted a perfect life and he wanted her to be in it with him.

She didn't want to go into her father's furniture business, neither did her brother. 'This business has been in the family for three generations how can we let it go?' her father had woefully said. She did feel rather guilty about not wanting to continue the family legacy but knew that she couldn't live up to her father's expectations. Eventually the business was sold and the lovely furniture and paintings were equally distributed between her and her brother.

Money wasn't an issue for her but she had an inquisitive nature and a good work ethic even though she was not academically gifted. She had never thought of having a serious career like a doctor or lawyer, she'd been too busy looking after her father and brother after her mother had died and her father had rather spoilt her financially but she desperately wanted some freedom and to get away from the confines of the family home and domesticity. She ended up with the job at the school. Lots of long holidays in which spend time with her friends and to support her newly widowed father so it suited them both.

When Sam first met Tim, he seemed so

dashing and full of energy. He was in the staff rugby team and it was obvious he was a good player; a nippy fly half in his number 10 jersey. She'd go and watch him play, stand at the side of the pitch and shout encouragingly when he had the ball. She loved to see him playing and there was no doubt she fancied him as she saw him leading the game, his powerful muscular legs looking strong and sexy. He was an assertive player and would do anything to get the upper hand on the opposing team. That's what separates rugby from any other sport in the world - the ability to knock the stuffing out of each other but then you shake hands after the match and return to being best friends as before. He had a combative streak which had been noted by some of his colleagues as maybe a tad aggressive.

When he was still relatively young he attained his ambition and secured the post of head teacher at one of the top boys public school and the family bought a house nearby. She took on another clerical job at that school and between them they ran a good show and were much liked by the boys and parents alike. They had done well together and even though they would have liked more children were content with their young son. Her health problems seemed to be under control and everything was good except for his workload and lack of time to spare for his family.

He did have a sense of humour though. So passionate was he about rugby that on several occasions he had quietly entered the school chapel and changed the hymn numbers displayed on the hymn boards ready for the next school service. It used to cause chaos and confusion between Mrs Palmer, the organist, and Mr Moore, the school chaplain, as the new numbers were actually the rugby scores. Mrs Palmer didn't know what she was meant to be playing and there would be a flurry of page turning with boys trying to find what hymn they were meant to be singing.

She truly tried hard to understand about his job and that it required a lot from him. She even tried to speak to him about his mood swings but he would just shrug and say, he was fine, which she knew he wasn't. One time when she had mentioned something she was upset about he seemed to take it as a criticism and became angry. He had grabbed her by the wrist with some force which had hurt her. She had genuinely felt frightened of him. It had happened a second time when he had been especially angry and stressed about a situation with one of the boys at school who had been found out sending explicit videos. He was going to have to expel the boy and was expecting the parents that afternoon. It was always difficult having to speak to parents about this sort of thing but he was in no doubt that the boy was a bad influence at the school and he would have to go but he seemingly took out his anger on his wife.

She was determined she should seek help. She was starting to think that maybe it was something she had done but her friends assured her she wasn't to blame. Perhaps, she thought, he was just too busy with other things and they should take a holiday.

Without his career they wouldn't have been able to live as comfortably as they did but then she began to think that he was choosing his work, sport, charity events, everything else over her. Yes, she had her job at the school, she had friends, hobbies and a child to look after but it was her husband's attention that she craved and he was never there when she was at home. When he did come back to the house he was becoming more critical of everything that she did and his mood swings and bad temper reached worrying levels. So many dinners were left uneaten and thrown away. So many invitations refused or cancelled because he was busy doing other things and wouldn't be able to make it. Sometimes she became annoyed because she felt that people could have invited her on her own when she had explained that he was busy. It meant that she had to sit at home whilst he was out and about and this all started to pall on her. He loved her and their son she knew that but what she wanted was his time. She was becoming more and more lonely and depressed.

Tim was totally absorbed in his work, meeting up with his old pal Mark to watch rugby matches and attending charity events but this still was not enough in his life, he wanted more. He had always been strongly religious right from childhood but now he felt as though God was guiding him in the direction of ordained ministry and he knew he would never feel truly fulfilled until he had pursued this calling. With such a strong urge to fulfil this he enrolled at theological college. He was away for long periods of time and Sam often felt lonely. She knew he was a workaholic when she married him, but his dedication to his career, his sport and now his religion were taking its toll on their marriage. She felt frustrated when he went with his friend Mark to watch sport. She tried to tell herself that it was good for him to have a friend to spend time with and talk about different things but really she felt he seemed to favour anything over coming home to spend time with her and their son.

Things all changed for her one gloomy late autumn morning. It had been a dreary start to the day at the school office with one problem after another. The computer system had been playing up and she couldn't get on with sending out a mailshot to all the parents, which was particularly tiresome. Anyway, as she was sitting there waiting for the IT chap to turn up and sort things out with the computers the father of one of the pupils came into the office. There had been a minor rugby accident at the school and he had come to collect his son to take him home.

He was tall and slim, well over six foot, had blonde hair and piercing blue eyes which seemed to penetrate her very soul when he fixed his eyes on her. He literally took her breath away with his looks and the way he spoke to her made her feel special and quite weak at the knees.

Whilst he was waiting for matron to bring the injured boy to the office he engaged in conversation with her. He was so easy to talk to and she found the worries of that morning slipping away. She already knew that he was a builder but he was telling her that he had a special interest in carpentry. She asked him, just out of interest, if he could fix some cupboards in the house.

'Certainly, give me your phone number and I'll give you a call and come and have a look to see what you want,' he had said.

True enough he phoned her within a couple of days and that was how the affair started. She felt young again, sexy and desirable. She knew it was wrong but it was exciting.

She had tried to resist his advances but when Tim then announced that he was going on a retreat with the college and would be away for her birthday that was the final straw.

CHAPTER THREE

There was a knocking at the door which woke her up. 'Josh has forgotten his key again,' she thought. Getting sleepily out of bed she unhooked her dressing gown from the back of the bedroom door and hastily flung it around her. She tied the belt as she stepped downstairs expecting to open the door to a smiling Josh apologising for getting her up and for forgetting his key yet again. That though is when her whole life changed and the moment that every mother dreads.

As she opened the door two police officers were standing on the doorstep and she instantly knew that something very bad must have happened. The police officers both clearly looked nervous.

'Are you Mrs White and do you have a son called Josh?'

'Yes, yes I do, is everything alright?' She knew instinctively, her mother's intuition coming into force that something major and terrible had happened to her son.

'May we come in please? We have some upsetting news for you.'

Posy invited them into the sitting room and they asked her to sit down. Fear and a feeling of nausea overcame her.

'We've been asked to come and see you to advise that your son has been in an accident on his motor bike.' The female police officer showed her a wallet and an ID card that Posy recognised as belonging to Josh.

Posy began to shake and the WPC held out a hand to help her to the sofa.

'He is alive and is being treated at the hospital where we picked up his wallet and ID. It seems as though he took a bend badly and came off his bike not very far from here. Luckily, someone drove past not long after and found him. They rang the police and the ambulance came and have taken him to the hospital. He was wearing a helmet which has helped and the hospital are doing their best to look after him but I have to warn you that he is very seriously injured.'

When Posy looked back on this terrible moment she didn't know how she had coped with it. It was obviously a survival instinct in the face of a crisis and she calmly said,

'Where is he? I'll go straight to the hospital.'

'We will take you there,' the sympathetic woman police officer said.

The journey to the hospital was a blur but all the way Posy was thinking about what could have happened.

She knew that Josh didn't take risks and was a careful motorbike rider but there again it could have been just a minor misjudgement on his part going around the bend and she felt she knew which bend it was. On their road there was a notorious black spot and despite warning signs there had been many accidents there in the past, a couple of them fatal. She would often go down that road and feel a sadness when she saw the flowers that had been placed there. They were a stark reminder to take that particular bend with caution.

On arrival at the hospital she was ushered into the Emergency Unit and taken to see Josh. He was hooked up to all kinds of machines with tubes and a monitor bleeping by the side of him. The doctor on duty quickly came in to see her and calmly explained the situation to her.

'I'm afraid it's not looking good; your son has suffered major internal injuries and we can keep him on the life monitor for a few weeks but he has had a catastrophic injury to his brain also. As his next of kin you have the decision as to how we go about things. It's very soon after the accident so we will try everything we can to save him but I have to warn you that I don't think it's a positive situation. I'm afraid it's a matter of you waiting and we'll see how things progress over the next few hours.'

Posy sat back in the chair, took a deep breath and thought about life, one minute everything is happy and seemingly normal and then in a blink of an eye things can change and will never be the same again.

She sat in the waiting room all night drinking endless cups of coffee from the vending machine that she didn't really want, but it gave her something to do to break the anguish of waiting for news. She tried to look at some of the magazines on the table and read every poster on the wall but she wasn't really taking anything in and just felt blank. She telephoned her best friend, Angharad, who she had known since school days. She managed to tell her what had happened through tear-clouded eyes, often breaking down and unable to speak.

'I'll be right over,' said Angharad.

Angharad had been a blessing to Posy when she'd split up with Terry and was like a sister to her. They lived within ten miles of each other and met up at least twice a week and spoke on the phone nearly every day. Within 20 minutes Angharad arrived at the hospital and rushed into the waiting room flinging her arms around Posy.

'Oh my God Posy. Beautiful Josh, that lovely boy. I just can't believe it. I pray to God he will be alright.'

'I'm afraid it's not looking good Angharad. The doctors have already warned me to expect the worst.'

The night seemed long and the waiting room dreary and clinical. All manner of people walked in each absorbed in their own dilemma or family trauma and not noticing or caring about the two anxious women huddled together on the cold, hard chairs waiting for news but fearing the worst. The TV, on in the background with no one taking any notice to whatever old, repeats were playing and the same news coming on every half hour with boring repetition. Posy didn't care what else was happening in the world. All she cared about was Josh and how he was. Being a nurse she had a good idea what was going on in the Intensive Care Unit and she knew that it didn't look good.

When the intensive care doctor asked to see her and took her into a small private room she felt a sense of impending disaster.

'Please take a seat. There is no easy way to tell you this. The monitor tells us that your son is actually brain dead and has no chance to ever recover or lead a normal life. His heart is still beating though as the ventilator is keeping it going. The ventilator is providing enough oxygen to keep his heart beating but without this it would stop,' he paused for a moment and took hold of her hand.

'This is an extremely sensitive subject but we note that he is on the Organ Donor Register and that it was his wish for his organs to be donated. We need to ask your permission for this to happen.'

Posy had known that Josh was on the Register as was she. They had decided this together and both of them had applied at the same time.

'Yes, I know that he is on the Register. That was his wish and I give my authorisation if you wish to use any of his organs. There are no other members of the family to ask, his father is in Australia and he has little contact with us, I am the only one. Let me just think about this for an hour or so, it's such a major decision and my head is spinning right now.' She said this with trembling breath her whole body shaking with the stress and realisation of what was happening.

'I'm afraid we don't have an hour for a decision to be made. If we want to keep the organ alive it has to be done within four hours.'

'Of course, I should have known that. I'm a nurse. I'm not thinking straight.'

Posy knew that she should contact her ex-husband but was too fraught to make the call. In the end she sent him a text to let him know the terrible news. She didn't want to face having to tell him or anyone else what had happened. He phoned her mobile within minutes and as she answered it she could hear that he was distraught and in floods of tears. Terry offered to get on the next plane to see them but Posy explained there would be little point as the situation was dire and it would serve no purpose him coming all this way just to get upset; there was nothing he could do. Did he consent to his son's heart being donated? Terry was in agreement to this and with great emotion and grief Posy confirmed with the doctors that she gave her consent, as his next of kin, for her son's heart to go to a recipient.

This all happened like something in a nightmare and she felt her life was being lived in slow motion. She was making moves and decisions that she never could have envisaged. She knew that Josh would not want to live like this, hooked up to monitors and being kept alive artificially. It was better to let him go with some dignity rather than prolong the inevitable.

Angharad hugged her tightly and said, 'It's your decision hun, and I know you will make the right one. I'll always be around for you, you know that.'

Posy knew about the procedure for transplant surgery from her nursing experience and that time was of the essence. Doctors would consult the donor waiting list and see who could be helped. They quickly informed her that there was a young man who needed a new heart as his own was badly diseased. He didn't live too far away and the organ could be taken to his nearest hospital for immediate transplantation. A transplant would save his life and this thought at least helped her to get through the pain and agony that she now inevitably would go through.

CHAPTER FOUR

She missed Josh so much. His presence, the sound of his voice, the smell of his clothes, the aftershave, Jean-Paul Gaultier, that she'd bought him with it's soft leathery fragrance with sweet, spicy and woody notes. She would never be able to smell that again without it invoking strong memories of her son, his good looks, his gentle good humour and kindly nature. The thought that she would never see him again was too much to bear and all around the house there were reminders of him and she felt his presence with her everywhere. It was as though she were on automatic pilot and getting up, getting dressed, having to eat were just motions without conscious thought.

She would speak to him out loud and once or twice she thought that she actually heard him answer.

'Am I going mad?' she asked herself. She

hoped that it was Josh speaking to her but in her logical mind couldn't rationalise with it. In her career as a nurse she had been present at many deaths. She felt that even though the life had gone from the body the soul was there somewhere. So many unexplained things. Who would have thought all those thousands of years ago that you could turn a knob and pictures and sounds would appear. The same was true with afterlife. Much more to be discovered although the sceptics, of course, would not have any of it.

She was intelligent enough to realise that it was the grieving process and that many strange thoughts and feelings would happen and she would never get over his death, hopefully it would just get easier to manage. It was much, much worse than when her parents had died. Your children were not meant to die before you. This was not the natural order of things. She had given birth to this beautiful human being and she would never get over the feeling of missing him.

The thought that his heart was still beating somewhere gave her hope to carry on with her life. She was comforted to a degree by the fact he had helped someone by his death and this was exactly the sort of person that Josh was and during the months that followed she tried to keep busy as much as she could. She only had a couple of weeks off from work and found that going back to work and keeping busy was the best thing that she could do. Sleeping helped and also by thinking about the good times she had had with Josh but she couldn't help being curious and speculating what the young man was like who had received his heart and how he was faring.

***

So many things happened during the first few months after Josh's death that she couldn't explain, like the times when his number came up on her phone when she hadn't dialled it.

Then there was the time when there had been a banging noise coming from her bedroom wall, a constant knocking she had never heard before. She didn't know if it was the pipes from the central heating, but the heating wasn't on so that didn't explain it. She couldn't fathom out what it was and then she realised what day of the year it was. It was Mother's Day. She had been aware that the day was coming up; she'd tried to avoid the hype and cards in the shop windows and was dreading it. Josh had always bought her such lovely Mother's Day cards and always made a fuss of her, but with everything else going on she had put it to the back of her mind. Now, it starkly dawned on her the relevance of the day and the strange noise that seemed to be calling for her attention.

'I know who that is,' she calmly said to herself. Far from being spooked by this she found it strangely comforting.

Unexplained things also happened to Josh's friend, Ben, who often popped around to see her just for a chat about things.

'You know, Mrs White, I think Josh sometimes plays a trick on me. I've had a couple of times when I've seen that there's a message from him, his name comes up on my mobile but there's no message there.'

Then, there was the time when she spotted something on the ironing board that looked like a little bit of old plastic. 'What is that?' she thought. On closer inspection it was the plastic name tag she had kept from the hospital when Josh was born. 'Baby White', with the date and time of his birth. How strange, and especially when she looked at the clock and it was 11.15am the exact time that he was born. Well, the time was obviously a coincidence but how could it have got there from my overhead cupboard where I keep all my precious things? At least it wasn't the actual date of his birthday - that would have been too much to get my head around, she thought.

Strange things happened but somehow it was oddly comforting, it felt as though Josh was keeping in touch with her. Friends, work colleagues and acquaintances tried to support her with suggestions of bereavement counselling, various groups she could join and hobbies to take up that might prove a distraction to her grief.

One well-meaning acquaintance encouraged her to start wearing orange. 'The sky takes on shades of orange during sunrise and sunset, orange is the colour that gives you hope that the sun will set only to rise again,' the well-meaning alternative soul had suggested to her. Nice try, thought Posy, but she didn't actually like the colour orange and it served only to make her look wan and slightly jaundiced.

Getting a dog, that was another kindly thought that someone had suggested and it was an idea that she had seriously thought about and she'd spent several evenings scouring the internet looking at cute puppies. She wondered what breed would suit her, a large dog, maybe a German Shepherd, or a small one? Perhaps a small one - West Highland Terriers were rather appealing. Of course, nothing could replace her son, but dogs were such loving, faithful creatures and good company. She had never owned a dog and, as a child, would have loved one but her mother had suffered with asthma so furry pets were out of the question. She put this idea on the 'maybe later' and 'when I'm not having to go to work' list - it would be cruel to go out all day and leave a little dog on its own.

Several people had suggested that she go and visit a medium. She didn't like the thought of that though and wanted to let Josh Rest in Peace. It wasn't good to interfere with spirits and besides which she felt it was creepy and unnatural.

Posy queried whether the loss of a loved one was a greater emotion than love itself but then the deeper the love the more deeply you felt the loss. What greater love is there than a mother for her child?

It was at this time that Posy decided she wanted to do something altruistic in memory of her son. There was nothing more that she could do for him physically now but conceivably some good could come out of this sorry situation. Yes, he had helped another young man to continue and enjoy a healthy life but Posy was inspired to raise awareness of the need for more donors and collect money for charities for this cause. In fact, she had a moment of inspiration and decided that she wanted to set up a charity in her son's memory. She had been shocked to read the statistics that 1 in 5 patients waiting for a heart transplant will die without receiving a transplant due to the shortage of an organ donor.

Her mind was in overtime with all the thinking and planning how she could make this dire situation into something good.

This will inspire me to carry on.

The first thing I'm going to do is open a separate bank account for my charity work and keep any money I raise in that until I find a worthy cause to give it to. Next I'm going to have a Garden Party and all funds raised will go to charity. Then I'm going to get the residents at the Care Home knitting and making things to sell. Some of them are really talented. One of the gentlemen I know is an accomplished artist and we also have one who is great at wood carving. It will give them an incentive to getting creative and will also be a positive recreation for them. I've got to start somewhere and we'll have a fund raiser there for staff and families. I'm going to make this into my project and set a goal to raise as much money as I can in memory of Josh.

With this in mind Posy felt a challenge before her and felt positive in her new project.

CHAPTER FIVE

Haydn seemed so healthy to begin with that they were shocked to find that he had inherited his mother's heart problem. He could live a normal life but as he got older symptoms would start to show and he would have a considerable chance of not living to see his 21st birthday. His mother had sadly died of heart failure when he was 19 and his father had been on his own since. His primary concern had been his son and his life revolved around his hospital appointments.

He had received amazing attention from the cardiac medical team but had to be careful what he did and not to do anything too strenuous which rather restricted his life. The only thing that could help him have a fulfilled life would be to have a heart transplant and he had been on the transplant waiting list for five years but there had been no suitable donor to date. When the hospital contacted him to say that there was a possible donor he was excited but it was with mixed feelings. It was tinged with sadness as this meant that someone else had given up their life but it could mean the start of a longer, healthier future for him.

The call came at 2.00 in the morning.

'Is that Haydn Woburn Smith? It's the Organ Donor Register here. We have you on the list awaiting a heart donor. We've been contacted as we have a possible heart donor match for you. Can you get to John Radcliffe Hospital within two hours?'

He felt a tremor of excitement and fear. The call he had been waiting for had finally come. He knew not to get too excited in case the heart wasn't a match but he felt hopeful and optimistic. He knew, however that his gain would also be someone else's loss and he was sensitive enough to acknowledge this. He had been prepared through counselling and knew what the procedure entailed.

He said to the caller that he would be able to get there as soon as he could. His father would drive him and it should easily be within an hour. It was the middle of the night and he knew there would be little traffic on the roads at this time. They had done this drive many times over the years for various appointments and timed it in expectancy for this moment.

'Go straight to the Cardiothoracic Services when you get there. Time is of the essence. We have four hours in which to operate.'

He'd had an emergency bag packed and ready during the years he had been waiting for this call and he'd visited the transplant clinic at the hospital every month for a check up and was well aware of the procedure he would be having.

He calmly went to his father's bedroom and woke him up to tell him that this could possibly be the time for the transplant that could so radically transform his life. They made the drive to the hospital in silence knowing that their gain was another family's loss and respectful of this fact but also aware that it had been someone's wish to help another life by being an organ donor.

The hospital were expecting him and once he'd had a few routine tests it was found that the donor's heart was a perfect match for him. As he was wheeled into the operating theatre and before the anaesthetic was administered all sorts of feelings and fears were fluttering around inside his mind. Feelings of anxiety, apprehension and worry mixed with the positive feelings of hope and perhaps a magical, miraculous rebirth into a healthy body and continuation to a long and happy life.

Would he survive this operation?

Whose heart was he receiving? So many things to worry about and then the anaesthetic took effect and he drifted off into oblivion whilst the surgeons practised their medical magic.

The operation was carried out swiftly and competently by a highly skilled team. He received his new heart and once it had started to beat for him the surgeons watched to see how it was working and made sure there were no leaky valves. So far so good, but he had a long way to go with recuperation and recovery.

He'd had strange dreams whilst he was under the anaesthetic. He dreamt vividly that he was walking down a country road. He walked around a sharp bend in the road and he saw flowers in a pile and a cross. Quite disturbing dreams but he was undergoing a major operation and pumped full of drugs so it wasn't too surprising.

When he awoke from the anaesthetic his eyes fluttered open and he saw his worried father and girlfriend sitting there watching over him. He felt groggy and slightly confused. It had all happened so quickly, over the course of 12 hours. He had been asleep in bed when the phone call had come calling him into the hospital and now here he was with a new heart and he could only try to imagine who the donor had been and what had happened. At the same time he felt elated. This was hopefully the start of a new, healthier life for him and the possibility of being able to do things that had been unavailable to him before. Yes, he knew that he would have to take medication for the rest of his life but this was a small price to pay for the gift of a healthy longer life expectancy.

His father tried to visit the hospital every day while he was recovering but missed a couple of times due to work pressures. That wasn't a problem for him, he was used to his father being busy and he had his devoted girlfriend on hand and she was there to assist with bringing him home. She was a great help to him and gave him the love and support he needed. When he came home there was a support system and a nurse came in to see him every day to check up on his progress and make sure everything was healing as it should. He was advised to take it easy for three months and greatly missed being able to do his gardening but was able to catch up on lots of other things on the internet and quite enjoyed the peace and quiet he was having. After a couple of weeks Haydn felt so much better. He didn't want to put his life on hold any longer and he'd had enough of resting and he started to go out into the garden and generally pottered around finding the fresh air and looking at everything coming into bud - very therapeutic.

It was spring and bulbs and green shoots were coming up and bursting into life and this is how he felt too, that he was coming alive again.

He had been given another chance of life and he felt thankful. He was eternally grateful to the person who had donated the heart which was now beating inside him. He had decided that he would write a thank you letter to the donor's family expressing his gratitude and this he did hoping that they understood how much he appreciated what their son had done for him.

CHAPTER SIX

Posy was a much valued member of staff at the care home and her fund raising ideas had breathed life into many of the residents at the care home who were now busily knitting, crocheting, painting, whittling and using many other skills to make items to sell. Posy hadn't quite decided on who would benefit from the proceeds yet, but the residents were delighted to help.

Although she knew she shouldn't have favourites there was one lady, Mrs Laney, who she was particularly fond of. She was an interesting person who had led a colourful life out in Singapore where she had lived with her husband. She'd been brought up in Singapore where her father had been a very successful rubber trader and then met her husband who had been a director of a large and prestigious banking corporation, that was still in business to this day. They had led a fantastic life out there and some of the exploits they got up to in those days were enough to make your hair stand on end. She would go to tea dances in the afternoons with her friends who were predominantly British, with a handful of Malay royalty and wealthy Chinese. The main activity was dancing but Mrs Laney told about the wonderful acrobatic shows that were put on by the cabaret artistes in the ballroom overlooking the sea. With the large picture windows open to the breeze the room was referred to as the 'coolest ballroom in the East'. Posy wasn't sure if the use of the word 'cool' meant the same thing in those days.

She also told Posy the story of how her and her husband were so well known in those days in Singapore that letters would sometime arrive at their house addressed only to The Laney's, c/o Singapore!

She recounted the story of how many years before a wild tiger had escaped and managed to creep into the comfortable confines of the billiard room at The Raffles Hotel and was cowering under the billiard table. Its presence was only discovered by a waiter who had come in delivering drinks. He raised the alarm and unfortunately it was shot five times before receiving a fatal blow. This was the last tiger ever to have been shot in Singapore, thank God. And to commemorate this in 1986, the Chinese year of the Tiger, a live tiger was brought into the Raffles Hotel where Mr and Mrs Laney were drinking with their friends at the time. They were drinking at the Long Bar, which was their favourite watering hole, and the tiger was lifted up and put on the billiard table. Mrs Laney had actually stroked that tiger, she told her. Of course, she'd had to have a few Singapore Sling cocktails after that to calm down her nerves.

They used to have long chats both enjoying the company and laughs they had and Mrs Laney knew all about Josh and his accident and the fact he had donated his heart to another young man. She told Mrs Laney how she'd received a lovely letter from the recipient of Josh's heart but it was anonymous and sent through the mediation team. She had been assigned an Organ Donation Specialist Nurse but all she would tell her was that a young man had received the heart and he seemed to be doing very well. She would love to know who it was and to even possibly hear that very special heart beating and giving life to someone who would have died without it. She didn't find that thought strange although she knew probably some other people might, instead it gave her a feeling of warmth and consolation.

'My dear you have been through every mother's worst nightmare. If it helps in any small way then I am sure we can do something about finding out who the recipient of your sons' heart is. There are always ways and means you know,' she said with a confident, knowing smile.

'You've met Richard my son, do you remember him?'

Of course Posy remembered Richard Laney, he wasn't the sort of man you could forget. She knew that he had been in the Special Forces and after his retirement had worked as a private detective. He was a tall, distinguished looking man with an upright back and a regimental air about him. He'd always been very pleasant if rather aloof to Posy when she'd met him on his visits to his mother.

'I'll ask Richard if he can find out the information you want, he has contacts in all sorts of places and I'm sure he will be able to discover who received your son's heart and where he lives. You must be discreet though dear, won't you. I don't want him to get into trouble, but my motto is "nothing ventured, nothing gained" and if this would help you in your grieving process then that is a good thing.'

The next time Richard Laney came to visit his mother he and Posy had a chat. They went out for a walk in the care home gardens and Posy explained the situation about her son. She had a feeling that his mother may already have told him but he was tactful and appeared as though this was the first time he had heard it mentioned. After some thought and a few pertinent questions he said he would be able to gather the information she required but he would have to be very discreet as these things were highly confidential, as she well knew.

'Give me a few weeks and I should have some information for you; how you go about contacting them then will be a matter for you to sensitively decide.'

'Of course, thank you so much for agreeing to do this. It will give me so much comfort to know who the person is. All the hospital will tell me is that it is a male, in his twenties and he is doing very well since receiving my son's heart. I have had a lovely thank you letter from the recipient but it was anonymous as they were advised by the counsellor not to give out their name. It was a joy to receive it though.'

Two weeks came and went. Posy resisted saying anything to Mrs Laney and she hadn't seen Richard Laney since their talk. She had either been off duty when he had called visiting his mother or it had been Mrs Laney's daughter she had seen.

She often tried to picture the person who had received Josh's heart and imagined what he looked like. If she did ever meet him would she like him? That could be difficult.

Nearly a month had gone by when she saw Richard Laney again at the care home. 'Hello Posy,' he said, 'is there a private room where we can talk, I have some positive news for you?'

Her heart beat faster in anticipation of what she was about to hear. Something made her feel slightly guilty, as if what she was doing was wrong, but on the other hand it felt only natural to want to know where Josh's heart was beating still.

'Yes, I'll take you into the office; I know that it's the secretary's day off and we can have some privacy there,' she said, her mind racing and feeling slightly giddy with excitement at the news she was about to receive.

Posy showed him into the nursing home office and in the corner of the room were two comfortable chairs and a circular table with a box of tissues placed on it. This room had been witness to many families receiving news regarding their loved ones, but Posy suspected there had been nothing compared to what she was about to hear.

Richard took a seat and as he did so pulled up the knees of his sharply pressed trousers. He was always so immaculately dressed with his starched white shirts and well cut blazer. She also noticed his highly polished brogues. Not a hair or stitch was out of place with Richard Laney. She guessed that his house must be impeccable too. I bet all his books are in alphabetical order she speculated and then, I wonder if he is married, and if he is, what his wife is like. So many questions and thoughts swimming around in her head.

He put some papers neatly on the table and cleared his throat before he said slowly and concisely, 'Are you ready for this information?' Posy nodded her head.

'I have found out the name and address of the young man who received your son's heart. He lives in a village in the Cotswolds with his father. I gather from the information I gleaned that he seems to be doing very well since his transplant. Please remember this is highly private information. The Organ Donor Service stipulate that protecting the anonymity of both the donor and transplant recipient is of paramount importance, so the information I will be giving you is not strictly meant to be given out. There is a process where you could have found out this information for yourself but it can be upsetting and quite emotionally charged. However, many people find that knowing who the recipient is does help with the grieving process and I am sure that this would be to your benefit. If I hadn't thought this my conscience would not have allowed me to trace the recipient for you.'

Richard Laney, handed over an envelope which she carefully opened. Inside was a sheet of thick vellum writing paper on which he had written in his carefully italicised handwriting the name of the recipient and his address. Posy picked up the piece of paper with unsteady hands and read it over three times, digesting the name and address and trying to picture the person who bore that name and how a major part of Josh now lived on through his donation.

'Thank you so much,' said Posy. She felt

like giving him a hug and a kiss for all his trouble but then thought better of it. I don't think he is the sort of person who would appreciate shows of emotion she speculated to herself. As she contained her feelings she said, 'I think I just need a bit of time to mull all this over and decide how I am going to process this information, if at all. When I feel like making contact a letter is probably a good way to start.'

'I agree,' said Richard, 'just take your time and you will know when the time is right. These things are very difficult emotionally but I am sure you will be sensible and I hope that you gain comfort from whatever you plan to do now that you have the information.' He gave her a kindly smile and to her amazement as they stood up to leave the room he turned to her and gave her a warm hug which was definitely not something she was expecting. You should never judge a book by its cover, she mused.

'My mother is very fond of you and I know she greatly enjoys talking to you. She was very distressed at what happened to your son and I've been happy to help you. Her stay here at the care home has definitely been made much more pleasant with your ministrations and nursing help so this is a sort of thank you. It is the least I can do.'

She said goodbye to Richard and went to find her bag to put the information safely away. She would have a closer look at it when she arrived home. She stopped off at the supermarket to get some things she needed. She tried to persuade herself that it was for necessary items but her main purpose of going there was to buy wine. She realised that she was depending on it more and more as a crutch to drown out the sorrow of the real world. She would open the bottle and more than likely pour herself a very large glass or two as soon as she arrived home. She was worried that she was drinking too much, it was every night now, but anything to get her through her pain and loss was her reasoning of an excuse.

CHAPTER SEVEN

The bottle of Sauvignon Blanc was already chilled and looked invitingly at her from the worktop. I'll just have a sip of this to calm myself, thought Posy, and she proceeded to open the bottle and pour herself a glass. She excitedly took the envelope that Richard Laney had given her from her handbag and settled down comfortably on the sofa taking a large glug of the delightfully fruity wine as she did so.

She looked at the piece of paper with the all-important name and address written on it. She would have to summon up the courage before she could do anything with the information she now held. She felt very alone and vulnerable at that moment. Nobody was going to help her unless she helped herself. She could ask Angharad to come with her to the address on the paper but she didn't want to share this experience with anybody else. Besides which she wasn't even sure how she was going to deal with things.

I'm just going to have to take the bull by the horns, she thought. I'm going to go there and find him.

She had consulted the map to see where the address of the recipient was. Google maps helped and she did hours of research on the internet. She was completely immersed in her quest and by the time she looked at the clock she realised that three hours had passed and she had finished the whole bottle of wine! I've definitely got to keep an eye on this drinking, she thought as she brushed her teeth in the bathroom before slumping into bed.

On her next day off she took the plunge and made the decision to at least go to the village where the young man lived.

In a way she felt that what she was doing was wrong, stalking even, but then again it felt like the most natural thing in the world to know who had her son's heart and she didn't care what other people thought. For once she was following her personal intuition and letting her heart rule her head and she would continue with her search. She had come this far in getting the name and address and now she couldn't let things rest.

She walked out of her house feeling

positive and flung her handbag over to the passenger's seat. She smiled to herself as she buckled up her seat belt and started the engine. She drove with some trepidation but also excitement, her heart beating so fast that she thought maybe she shouldn't be driving. Was it safe to drive when she was in this frame of mind? Hell yes, life can be hard and this is something that I have to do. I need to find where my boys' heart is. I know this isn't unreasonable, just passionate and I have to do it.

As she was driving she felt as though she was in a dream, as though she was on remote control with the car seemingly driving itself down the motorway. When the Sat Nav told her to take the next exit off the motorway she felt relief, she had never liked motorway driving and felt threatened by lorries and always stayed in the slow lane, only overtaking when absolutely necessary and then going back to the slow lane as soon as she could.

'I don't care if it annoys other people,' she said out loud, 'after what I've been through, I just want to get there safely and as far as I'm concerned I have all the time in the world.'

On she went through the market town of

Cirencester and then she continued through a small village.

This is all very pretty, she thought. She never went on holidays abroad and liked to stay within the familiar shores of England but Gloucestershire was not a county that she had visited or if she had it had just been a drive-through. She drove down a long tree lined road, which seemed to go on for miles. It looked as though it was most likely owned by the Forestry Commission and the trees were tall pines towering by the side of the road which made it dark and foreboding in their shade.

She knew she was nearing her destination when she reached another small village with a row of honey-coloured stone cottages with steeply pitched roofs on either side of the road that were probably workers cottages in days of old but now most likely housed well-heeled professionals. She imagined that property in this area would not be cheap.

There was a pub with a picture of a roaring lion which said 'The Lion' underneath. Over the road was a church. The sacred and the secular were divided here by only a road and very handy for that quick one after church and before Sunday lunch.

'You have reached your destination,' the Sat Nav authoritatively informed her.

She turned down a lane by the side of the church and there were three large houses all built of the traditional Cotswold stone with mullioned windows. She had memorised the name of the house she wanted to find, Church House, and there it was with a pale blue front door, lion-head door knocker and a low, stone wall shielding the house from the lane. Posy stopped the car in front of the house to have a closer look. An array of white and red roses were tumbling over the wall and a lilac tree was in full flower. The grass on the verge was newly mown and a bay tree stood neatly either side of the entrance gate.

She drove round to the church and parked her car in the car park there. The sign said 'St Mary's Church' and she looked over to the church beyond which had a typical, square, Norman tower. She walked through the graveyard which had many old tombs and headstones, some with beautifully carved cherubs and symbolic figures of past centuries. She saw an old sundial on the south wall and managed to read the time at 12.15 or near enough, she guessed. After wandering around the graveyard and taking time to read a few of the old inscriptions on the gravestones she decided to enter into the lovely old building.

She looked forward to stepping into the safe haven of the church and being able to reflect on her feelings, perhaps envisage that Josh was still with her but knowing this was not possible. However, his heart was still beating and she fully intended to hear that beat again albeit in another body.

Posy had once been a devoted church-goer but life's ups and downs had made her question her religious beliefs and she couldn't relate to anything religious now. She had toyed with Buddhism and even Wicca once upon a time but life had been busy and she felt that she didn't need this in her life. When Josh was a baby and she was still together with her husband they had him christened but really, when she thought about it, was it because of any strong beliefs or just a good excuse for a party? She had taken Josh to Church up until he was about nine. He would trot off to join the other children at Sunday school but then the visits to church had petered out when he started to protest about getting ready in his Sunday best and made it very obvious that he no longer wanted to go.

Now, however, even though she was no longer a believer she felt that she needed the sanctuary and peace of the beautiful, old church and she wandered down the paved church pathway, the carefully tended graves and freshly cut grass in between them lending an air of tranquillity to her state of mind. She imagined all the people who had trodden this path before her. People on their way to be married, people attending christenings and funerals of their loved ones. The complete circle of life for local families who would have walked this well-trodden path that she now took towards the church.

She entered through the porch and opened the solid, arched oak door carefully lifting the heavy iron handle. As she pushed the door open she felt a sense of calm overtake her, that familiar smell of old buildings: a mixture of damp, wood and candle wax. She wandered around the old church taking in the 13th century font and memorials to village families dating back several centuries. The sun's rays glinted through the stained glass windows; the beautiful blues, greens and reds casting twinkling shafts of coloured light onto the flag stoned floor. Two wrought iron plinths stood either side of the nave holding a colourful array of flowers. Roses, hydrangeas, delphiniums and trailing ivy cascaded over the sides. Someone had obviously taken a lot of trouble and had a great sense of design and colour to put this artistic display together.

Posy knelt down at one of the pews and said a silent prayer.

'Please God, whoever and wherever you are, give me a sign that my Josh is fine and resting in peace. I feel so close to him here and I know that his life was a happy and well lived one. Although cut short far too early he had done so much and had so much to look forward to. I don't want his life to have been in vain.'

She began to cry; she'd had all these months of grief and missing Josh she felt as though she had wept a sea of tears. When she lifted up her head she saw the copy of the Holy Bible and the hymn book in front of her. Her mother who had been a religious person used to open the Bible at a random page and hope she would find inspiration in the text that she read there. Posy, although she had found her mother's idea curious, now picked up the Bible and thought she may as well try her mother's method. She opened the Bible and casting her eyes upwards she placed her finger randomly on the page she had opened.

Revelation 21.4 'He will wipe every tear from their eyes. There will be no more death or mourning or crying or pain, for the old order of things has passed away. Posy felt angry. She snapped the Bible shut. This isn't the order of things; children aren't meant to die before their parents. I wish I could find inspiration but this hasn't helped at all. Maybe I've interpreted it wrongly. Perhaps someone could explain what this means to me but the way I'm feeling at the moment I don't get it.

She sat there for nearly half an hour feeling despondent but trying to come to terms with her thoughts in the space of the church. She had tried grief counselling but she wanted to deal with things in her own way. No one can tell another how to grieve. Each and every individual has to find their own way to cope with bereavement and it is an intensely individual emotion. Nothing could ever bring her son back and she just had to get on with her life and accept the blow that fate had dealt her. She felt close to Josh here in this temple of peace. Eventually she wiped away her tears, stood up and had a final glance around the church.

She heard the door open and she turned

around to see a man who had entered the church. He was probably in his late 40s, maybe early 50s, about 5 foot 10 inches tall, of fairly stocky build, with dark hair going grey at the temples and deep, brown eyes. He walked over to the Bible stand at the top of the Church and carefully turned some of the pages and placed the bookmark at his selected choice. As he walked down the aisle he glanced towards Posy.

'Good afternoon,' he said jovially to her, then he looked more closely at her and perceptively noted that she had been crying.

'Are you alright?' he asked kindly.

'I've just been having a look around this lovely church. It's so peaceful and I… I… oh I'm so sorry,' she broke down in tears.

'I'm so sorry,' she said, 'it's just that I lost my son a few months ago and all the pain and sadness has just come flooding to the surface whilst I have been sitting here saying a quiet prayer.'

'I'm the Vicar here, Tim. Please stay for as long as you wish and make the most of this quiet space. I'm just going to make a cup of tea in the kitchen, would you like one? And, if you're lucky there might be a piece of Mrs Wilson's famous coffee and walnut cake in the tin if you'd fancy a piece.'

'That would be lovely, thank you so much,' Posy replied.

Minutes later, he came back with a mug of tea and a piece of cake and held them out for Posy to take. She took a sip of her tea and a bite of the cake.

'This cake is delicious,' she said as she savoured the mild coffee flavour and the sweetness of the icing. She took a walnut from the icing and popped it into her mouth not really thinking about what she was doing but the crunchy texture of the walnut and taste of the icing were comforting to her.

'How old was your son?' he asked gently.

'19,' she replied, 'he died in a motorbike accident.'

'I have a son who is 25,' he responded, 'He has been very ill and nearly died a while back so I have some idea of how you are feeling.'

'What was wrong with him?' Posy asked.

'He had a heart condition but thankfully and thanks to God, he had a heart transplant four months ago and has been doing so well. It's still early days but it has made such a difference to his life that hopefully he will be able to work and enjoy life to the full which he was never able to do before.'

Posy looked at him incredulously, as the penny dropped. 'Do you live at Church House?' She asked Tim.

'Yes, it is owned by the ministry. I've been here for five years now and I hope I'm here until my retirement.'

'Oh my God, it's you I have travelled here to see, your son has my son's heart!' exclaimed Posy, 'I know I shouldn't have but after I received the thank-you letter from your son, I traced where he was living and I drove here today but didn't know what to do next. I felt so lost. Please forgive me if you think I have done the wrong thing.'

Tim looked at her his face not betraying any emotion, and calmly said, 'I totally understand your feelings. I know my son wrote to the family of his donor through the Mediation Service and I would have liked to have thanked you personally as well but knew that it wasn't standard practice to find out where you were and contact you. In my position as a minister I have to be careful to comply with regulations as anything else could be deemed as highly irregular and I could face disciplinary charges. You have given up so much and losing your precious son has been heartbreaking for you. It is the worst thing in the world that could possibly happen to a parent to lose a child. Believe me I do understand and I am so pleased to have met you.'

Posy looked at him, she could see that he was visibly moved at meeting her and he had great compassion in his eyes.

'Would it be possible to meet your son?' she asked with trepidation, her voice audibly wavering.

'I will have to ask him. His name is Haydn. We will have to deal with this very sensitively as it could be a shock for him. He is making such a good recovery that I don't want to upset him. Let me have your email address and I will contact you shortly after I have spoken to him and let you know how he feels. I am sure that he will want to see you but best if I check. Are you alright to drive home? Where do you live, is it far away?'

'It's about a two hour drive but I guess I could have done it a lot quicker. I'm rather a cautious driver you see and prefer to take it slowly. It's not a bad drive and the last hour was beautiful down all these country lanes, it is so beautiful around here.'

'I know I'm very lucky to have secured a position in this Parish. There were plenty of inner-city parishes I could have been assigned to but I really wanted somewhere in the country primarily for my son's health and also he loves gardening. I've been in teaching all of my career. I eventually became headmaster of a boy's school in the Cotswolds and then I felt the call to join the Church and after studying four years at theological college I then became ordained as a Vicar and joined this Parish. Church House comes with the job. It's a marvellous place to live and I hope if the Church can still afford to keep the house I'll be able to stay here until I retire. I have a house where I used to live when my wife was alive not too far away which is rented out. When I retire I'm not sure where I'll end up. I most likely won't go back to living there.'

'I'm sorry to hear that you wife has died. You've suffered a great loss too, that must have been hard for you. Do you have any other children?'

Tim looked away, not making eye contact with her.

'No, no, I have no other children, only Haydn. It's a long story.'

Posy could tell that he didn't want to discuss this line of conversation any more and they exchanged email addresses and phone numbers with the promise that Tim would contact her after he had consulted with Haydn whether he wished to meet with her.

The drive back didn't seem as long as it took to get there. Posy was in a world of her own, going over and over in her mind the coincidence of meeting the recipient's father in the church, the fact that he was a Vicar and her boldness in making the decision in the first place to try and find him.

Posy arrived back home, tired after her journey both physically and emotionally. It still seemed strange coming back to an empty house and not calling out to Josh or hearing his music playing. It was still early days in the grieving process and she felt as though she would never be able to feel truly happy again. I have to take care of myself she thought. There is no one else to and I need to keep going in memory of Josh.

She made herself a cheese and pickle sandwich and poured a glass of wine which went down quickly and almost subconsciously. The bottle was beckoning and before she settled down on the sofa she poured herself another larger glass. Just to keep me going she convinced herself. When she woke up the next morning she had a slight headache but took an aspirin and went to work as usual.

CHAPTER EIGHT

It was only the day after she had met Tim that she received an email from him.

Dear Posy
It was lovely to meet you yesterday and you were very brave to drive here on your own in the hope of meeting the recipient of your son's gift. I have spoken to Haydn - he is so grateful to you and your son and would love to meet you. Would you like to come up next weekend to meet him? I have a wedding to perform on Saturday at noon and I'll be busy for a couple of hours so anytime after 2.00 will be fine. You are very welcome to bring a friend if you think that would give you support or I can arrange for one of our Parish members who is a trained counsellor to be present. Please let me know how you would like to proceed and believe me, we owe you and your son so much.
Kind regards

Tim Woburn Smith
Vicar St Mary's Parish Church, Bolingbroke

Posy read and re-read the email several times. Time to seize the day, she thought. I'll tell him I will go up there on Saturday and I'm looking forward to meeting Haydn and I so hope that he's well and will continue to be. I think his suggestion of having a counsellor present is a good idea too but I'll ask Angharad if she will come with me as well, I think I need as much support as I can get.

Posy sent the email and then tried to calm herself. She telephoned Angharad to tell her the news and Angharad dutifully agreed to come with her next Saturday, offering to drive as she knew Posy was a nervous driver.

On Saturday Angharad arrived at Posy's house. She came in and they had a quick cup of coffee to steady the nerves before they set off.

'Posy hun, I hope you're feeling strong, this is going to be quite an emotional day for you. I think you're incredibly brave. Just let me know if it gets too much for you at any stage and I'll be there to help out however I can. To be honest I feel nervous too. I loved Joshua so much. Well, I was around since he was a tiny baby wasn't I and watched him grow up. We've been there for each other through so much.'

The friends had met at high school. It had been difficult for Angharad starting at a new school when her parents had moved from Wales and she had been bullied by some of the other girls over her Welsh accent but Posy had taken her under her wing and looked after her. They became firm friends and had shared births, deaths of parents, marriages and divorces; two marriages and two divorces in Angharad's case. Thankfully she was now ensconced with a man who Posy approved of and he seemed like a solid anchor in Angharad's life.

Jeff was the owner of a local garage and she had met him when she'd taken her car in for a service. They'd been together for three years now and it still seemed to be blossoming. It was very handy too as he gave Posy a discount on her annual car service and he'd managed to get a good deal for the motorbike that she'd bought for Josh, although that was rather a regretted purchase now.

They settled themselves in the car, set up the Sat Nav and off they went. Angharad had bought a bag of humbugs for the journey and

Posy was so nervous that she ate nearly the whole bag herself hoping to comfort her nerves for the impending meeting.

They drove down the same route that Posy had taken the previous week but this time it took thirty minutes less with Angharad driving and not afraid to take the fast lane and overtake anything that was in her way. She was a confident driver and enjoyed her new red Audi Sports car to the full that Jeff had found for her at a good dealer's price.

When they arrived outside Church House, Angharad turned off the engine and leant towards Posy. 'Are you sure you're ready for this, hun?'

'Absolutely, I've never been more sure of anything in my life.'

The two friends walked up the garden path and Angharad confidently gave three loud knocks with the brass lion-head door knocker. The door was opened by a lady who introduced herself as Mandy Melrose. She addressed herself to Angharad and explained that she lived in the village and was a trained bereavement counsellor.

'Vicar Tim asked me if I could be present as he thought it would be helpful to have someone else around, but I see you've brought a friend with you.'

'Actually it's me, I'm Josh's mum,' said Posy, suddenly finding her voice and stepping forward to the door. 'I would like you to be there with us as well so please stay and thank you for being here.'

Mandy led them through the hall into what must have once been an elegant sitting room. There were books everywhere but through the slightly haphazard untidiness Posy could see that the furnishings had obviously been chic once but looked rather shabby now. There were some lovely good quality pieces of furniture that looked possibly antique. There was a beautiful chest of drawers with inlaid mother of pearl and brass. There were many paintings hung around the room that looked to be either oil or watercolour originals.

In the middle of the far wall was a large fireplace with a wood burner, and above was an oak lintel. The large windows were framed with floral chintz curtains, and swags and tails framed the window. The look was very Laura Ashley from the 1970s, but it was a look that she liked.

'I'll go and make a cup of tea and call Tim and Haydn,' said Mandy and off she went leaving them settling down on the comfortable, squishy, cushion laden sofa and taking a good look at their surroundings.

There was a sound of a door slamming and then footsteps across the oak panelled flooring. Posy looked up to see a young man with blue eyes and a shock of ginger hair walking into the room. He was medium height and of slim build. He was wearing the usual uniform for young men of his age: jeans, checked shirt and trainers, the sort of thing Josh had worn. As her eyes skimmed over him, taking in this boy, this young man whose heart she felt belonged to her, she noticed that he had lovely hands with slim, creative fingers. He didn't look like his father with his ginger hair and fair skin and Posy speculated this trait must have come from his mother's side.

'Hello, Mrs White, I'm so pleased to meet you,' he said extending his hand with impeccable manners towards Posy.

'Please call me Posy,' she said when she felt able to speak, the tears welling up in her eyes. He had Josh's heart but, of course, he would never be Josh or could take his place but he had such an important part of him that was beating and keeping him alive.

They sat down and his father came into the room. 'How is everyone, are you alright Posy?'

She introduced Angharad and once introductions had been made all round things became less formal. For Posy it was the most difficult because of her loss. Haydn had gained from her son's death and for that she took comfort and felt a sense of calm.

Mandy sat in the armchair and looked concerned. She explained that she was there in her capacity as a counsellor and this situation wasn't something she had encountered before. She had worked in London previously and become disheartened by the increasingly cut throat tactics of corporate life. She had then turned her life around completely after several family members and friends had died. She had trained with a hospice in Oxford and been helping there for around five years now. She had a great level of compassion and understood her job well. She had met Tim at the hospice and he would contact her if any of his parishioners needed help with their struggle to come to terms with the loss of a loved one. Mandy knew that Tim had lost his wife suddenly and she had tried to talk to him about it but had hit a blank wall. He had been very abrupt with her when she had asked about his wife early on in their friendship and she sensed that this was something he definitely did not want to talk about which she found rather difficult to understand.

After an uneasy silence and chinking of tea cups as they had tea and cake, Posy had to stop herself from nervously laughing when she thought of the phrase "More tea vicar?" She was relieved when the telephone rang in another room and Tim excused himself to go and answer it. Posy felt herself relaxing a little. She felt that he was rather domineering and the way he watched her she found unnerving. He was charming, yes, and she thought he seemed a lovely man but it all seemed rather contrived and she started to feel as though it hadn't been a good idea to visit.

Haydn looked rather uneasy too and eventually stood up and asked 'Would you like to see the garden? I've been working on it ever since we moved here and I think I've done a pretty neat job so far. It's my pride and joy.'

He took Posy and Angharad outside to show them around the garden. Mandy followed them but left a discreet distance. She .

was there if they needed her. Tim stayed inside.

Haydn walked them around the garden. It certainly was beautiful. Numerous incumbents who had lived there had put their mark on the place and dotted about were some interesting old statues. Stone steps led up to a top lawn. Posy counted them as they walked up, five steps. When they were at the top lawn she could see a small pond, which Haydn informed them, had been one of his new additions. A little fountain was spouting water and there were a few koi carp happily swimming around, darting underneath the pond weed, the sun catching their golden scales as they came in to the light.

'This is so beautiful,' said Posy.

'Yes, it's a very old garden but I hope that I've added to some of its splendour,' said Haydn.

Posy thought that he sounded much older than his years. He was obviously a very creative and thoughtful young man with a definite artistic flair.

'I've been told by doctors to take it easy all my life and that I couldn't play the sport I really wanted to do or anything too taxing so I've cultivated a love of gardening. I know my father was disappointed that I couldn't play rugby. Very disappointed in fact.' He looked downwards and Posy could see that he felt he hadn't lived up to his father's expectations.

'I went to college in Devon where I did a two-year course in horticulture and landscape gardening. I loved it and I have a degree now and plan to set up my own business.'

'Well you've done an amazing job here,' Angharad interjected.

'It's just that I hadn't been well enough until now to really try and do something for myself. I planned and planted the garden at our old house in the next village and since dad's been the vicar at Bolingbroke I've taken on the task of looking after the garden here. There was a gardener who had been looking after this garden for years but he was bent double with rheumatism and eventually had to give it up. I've happily taken it on. There's nearly two acres in total. I've made an Elizabethan knot garden and also dug a vegetable patch where I grow most of the vegetables we eat. No more going to Tesco's,' he laughed. 'I've also planted a red and white flowerbed. I just love it and I spend every available moment I have out here working in the garden. It's so good for the body and the soul.'

Posy could see that this was a sensitive, young man who had had to deal with many situations in his life and she admired the way that he had dealt with life's challenges by channelling this through his love of nature.

'Do you do all this on your own?' Posy marvelled at the beautiful garden.

'I used to,' and here Haydn blushed slightly, 'but I met a girl at Horticultural College called Chloe, she has a degree in landscape gardening and has started her own business that she runs in Budleigh Salterton. It's a bit of a drive but she comes up here whenever she can and she helps me. Dad doesn't mind if she stays as it's nearly three hours for her to get back and she'll stay for the weekend and help me in the garden. It's not all work though as we do go out to the pub and go for long walks in the forest nearby.'

They went back into the house and Tim and Haydn asked to see photos of Josh which she proudly showed them on her phone. She was making a great effort in trying to keep strong and she felt as though she was coping with things remarkably well. Shortly afterwards

Posy felt the strain of the day had taken its toll on her, she was feeling weary and announced that it was time they should go home.

'We are so indebted to you and your beloved son Josh, his spirit lives on, its been wonderful to meet you,' said Tim.

'Please come and visit us whenever you wish. We always have things going on in the village. In fact, next Monday we're having a fête in the garden for the late August Bank Holiday weekend which is always fun so you'd be very welcome to join us all.' Posy thanked Tim and said she would think about it and let him know.

She then turned to embrace Haydn and as she did so her hand gently caressed over where his heart was. 'May I?' she said hesitatingly, 'may I just listen to your heart beating?'

Haydn brought her closer to him and placed her head by his heart and she could feel Josh's heart beating inside his chest. Even though he was no longer here he had given Haydn the gift of life and through this he lived on and had brought them together.

***

'Oh Posy, what a delightful young man,' said Angharad of Haydn, 'and the dad's not bad either, sexy vicar mmm!'

'Honestly Angharad, you are awful,' exclaimed Posy, but had to admit that she was thinking of those kind, brown eyes and he certainly had something about him that she warmed to. She kept thinking about him and Haydn all the way home.

CHAPTER NINE

Posy decided she'd go along to the fête the following Bank Holiday Monday and informed Tim of her decision.

'That's great,' he said, 'I'll be pretty busy though but hopefully will have some time to be able to spend with you. In fact, why don't you stay over then you won't be worried about having to drive back at the end of the day. We usually end up going to the pub for a few drinks afterwards and you can really relax. We 'only' have five bedrooms and with just the two of us living here and sometimes Chloe there is plenty of space. I'll get my lady who does to make up the bedroom for you.'

Posy made the drive to the Cotswolds with no problem. She was getting used to the drive and feeling more relaxed about things. She arrived at the village and there was plenty of action going on. It was obviously a big event for the village and the surrounding areas. Tourists had evidently heard about it too and the whole village seemed to be buzzing with people.

There had been a great effort made throughout the village and bunting was festooned around the houses. There was a scarecrow competition and everywhere she looked she could see some straw man dressed up, peeking around a bush or propped up against a lamp post. She had to laugh at some of them. There was a cowboy with a stetson and cowboy boots, and one that was supposedly meant to be Tim with a vicar's collar and black cassock.

She parked her car and walked up to the house. She could see Tim in the garden busily rushing around, organising things and pointing to where people should put their stalls. Nancy and Haydn were there too and there was a flurry of activity getting ready for the 1.30 start.

As soon as Tim saw her he rushed over to her and gave her a warm handshake. 'Welcome, welcome,' he greeted her.

'Can I hand you over to Haydn to show you to your room I just have to organise some of the stalls and then we've got Vicky Butler coming with a couple of her ponies to give rides. I'll have to sort out where we put them.

I want to make sure they're not anywhere near Haydn's flower beds or he'll kill me.' He raced off and left her in the welcoming hands of Haydn.

She was pleased to see that Haydn looked so well. His cheeks were glowing and his lips looked a healthy pink colour. She also thought he had put on some weight since she had last seen him and generally he looked much healthier, in fact he appeared to be blooming.

He greeted her warmly and put his arms around her. She instantly felt a connection with him. Yes, he had her son's heart so there was that very special bond there but she also liked him as a person. She was so grateful for that. It would have been difficult if she hadn't felt this way.

Haydn picked up her bag and led her into the house. As they walked into the hall she looked around at the oil paintings, one of which was of a young girl, probably around nine years old. She had long red hair, creamy skin and was wearing a blue and white checked dress and holding a white teddy bear.

'What a lovely painting,' she commented.

'Yes, that was my mother when she was a child, she was very pretty wasn't she? Most of the paintings we have here belonged to her or her family. We didn't want to leave them at our house whilst it was rented out. Some of them are quite valuable, I think. My mother's family had a furniture manufacturing business hence that's why there's all the lovely stuff that we have here. We've let our old house out unfurnished. I don't think dad ever wants to go back there though. He couldn't wait to leave it after my mother died.'

'She must have been a very beautiful woman, your mother,' said Posy, 'she was such a lovely looking little girl.'

'Yes, she was a lovely person too. Hold on a minute, I've got something for you,' said Haydn. He went off for a moment, leaving her standing there eyeing her surroundings. When he came back he had something behind his back which he then held out to her. It was a small bunch of flowers beautifully tied up with blue ribbon. 'I've cut these for you. I grew them myself,' he said, 'a posy for Posy.'

Posy felt the colour rise in her cheeks as she was visibly touched by this kind gesture.

'Oh thank you so much. What a lovely thought, they are beautiful. My real name is actually Rosalind, from Shakespeare's play As you like it. My mother had wanted to be an actress and never had the chance to fulfil that dream. My father didn't really like the name Rosalind. He thought it was too posh so he used to call me Rosy Posy and the Posy part seemed to stick. I love the blue ribbon.'

'Actually, the ribbon to tie around the posy was Chloe's idea,' said Haydn honestly, 'I wouldn't have thought of that detail,' and he gave a little laugh. 'Now, come on and I'll show you to your room and you can freshen up before the fête starts. Chloe is upstairs already unpacking, she's just driven up from Devon so I'll be able to introduce you to her too. She's really looking forward to meeting you and also to relaxing for a few days. She has had so many commissions for her garden designs just lately and her business is really taking off.'

He led her up the central staircase and along a corridor. The room she was shown into must have been lovely once but was rather run down now. The carpet was threadbare with a large what looked like a burn mark next to the bed. The curtains which would have been made from a brightly coloured flower-patterned chintz were sun-faded now and more shabby than chic. The bed when she lay down on it sagged in the middle but still felt comfortable enough for a decent night's sleep. Being a nurse, Posy had learnt to sleep wherever she could and she had no problem with doing that. She could sleep on a dining room chair if there was nowhere else. On one side of the window there was a small washbasin with a clean towel next to it, a small bar of soap and a tooth mug. Posy filled the mug with water and carefully took the blue ribbon from the small bunch of flowers so it wouldn't get wet. She smelt the flowers, the little pink roses giving off a most pleasant scent, and placed the little display on the 1930's-style dressing table. She wound the blue ribbon around the tooth mug to complete the effect. She washed her hands and splashed some water on her face. It was a balmy, late August day and she felt hot and sticky after her drive. Haydn hadn't shown her where the bathroom was but she guessed it was along the corridor and she'd have a look for it in a moment.

Posy looked out of the window on to the garden at the back of the house. She had a good view from there of the stalls laid out for the fête She could see the red and white flowerbed that Haydn had pointed out the last time she was here and further along she could see the Elizabethan-style knot garden that he had been helped with by Chloe. It looked spectacular from the bedroom window as she looked down on it, obviously in its early stages but she could see how it would grow and take shape over the years for future generations and inhabitants of the house to enjoy. She could make out various herbs that had been planted in between the intricately planted box hedges forming the shape of several knots. That is quite some design, she thought, I think they will both go a long way in their chosen profession if they continue with designs like that.

There was a large mahogany wardrobe in the corner of the room. Posy had not brought much with her as she was only staying one night but she had packed a summer dress just in case she needed to dress up. She opened her small overnight case and shook out her gently crumpled dress. She opened the wardrobe door to hang it up only to find that it was full of dresses already.

She caught a musky scent of old perfume, the smell you had sometimes in a charity shop. Perfume from years ago, the memories of nights out, celebrations and other people's lives that lingered on in that olfactory sense. Smell could invoke so many feelings. She was surprised and rather perplexed to see all these dresses hanging up especially in a male dominated house but there were a spare couple of hangers and she hung her dress on one.

Curiosity getting the better of her she had a closer look at the garments. They were obviously of good quality and appeared to be mostly silk in beautiful colours. She looked at a couple of the labels, she recognised that they were designer names and they were small, a size 8. She pulled one of the dresses out of the wardrobe on its hanger. It was tiny. There was no way she could have fitted into any of these dresses as she was a size 12 and always had been.

She speculated that these must have been Haydn's mother's clothes but found it rather strange as she knew that she had never lived in this house. Tim and Haydn had moved in after Sam had died so she wondered what the explanation could be to have them here. Or perhaps they belonged to Haydn's girlfriend, Chloe, that could explain it. They didn't look like the sort of dresses a twenty-something would wear but she had never met Chloe, perhaps she liked vintage clothes, a lot of younger people did. On either side of the hanging space there were shelves with neatly packed shoe boxes and handbags in cloth covers. She wanted to have a closer inspection of these things but felt that was rather intrusive so she went back to unpacking her few bits and pieces and went off in search of the bathroom.

Posy walked along the corridor. One of these rooms must be the bathroom, she thought. She had opened one door which was the airing cupboard, another which was a small single room and then the third door she opened to find there was a young woman there, who was unpacking a small suitcase that was placed on the bed.

'Oh I'm so sorry,' said Posy, 'I was looking for the bathroom.'

The girl was in her early twenties, she had long dark hair, was slim and wearing jeans and a T-shirt.

'Hi, I'm Chloe and I guess you must be Posy?' She had a warm and welcoming soft Devonian accent.

'Yes, that's right I'm Posy and thank you so much for my posy, very apt, that was a lovely thought.'

'It's wonderful to meet you. It must be hard coming here and seeing Haydn what with losing your son. I am so sorry for your loss. It has made such an incredible difference to Haydn's life and hopefully, in some small way, your son can live on in him. I have seen such an improvement in him since the transplant and every week he seems to be getting stronger and more positive.'

She gave Posy a heartfelt hug and Posy felt a wave of upset mixed with pride come over her. Her feelings were all over the place and she never knew if or when she would ever feel normal again. I guess this is the new 'normal' now. Never in her wildest dreams could she have imagined this situation. It all seemed so bizarre but this was life and it was happening.

'I've finished sorting my stuff now so I'll show you where the bathroom is. It's a bit old fashioned I'm afraid.'

Posy followed Chloe down the corridor and she opened the last door by the stairs to reveal a large but antiquated bathroom. The bath could do with re-enamelling, she thought.

'Just a word of warning,' said Chloe, 'start running the bath at least twenty minutes before you want one, it's rather slow to fill. There is no shower.'

'Okay thanks, I'll remember that,' laughed

Posy.

'I think Tim has an en-suite in his room but this is the only other bathroom in the house. There are two loos downstairs though which helps!'

As they walked downstairs Posy mentioned the clothes in the spare bedroom to Chloe and asked if they were hers.

'Oh no, they're not mine, they're Haydn's mothers. She never lived here but I guess the removal people just picked up the whole wardrobe and put it on the lorry with all the other furniture. It is a bit creepy though I find. I used to stay in that room when I first started visiting the house. To be honest I don't think Tim even knows that they are there. He's probably never even been in that room. He's so busy with parish life and all his charity work. He has a woman called Mrs Chiltern who comes in once a week to clean and do the laundry and Tim has nothing else to do with the house apart from shopping and cooking a bit. He seems to be quite spoilt by a lot of the parishioners though and is always being given pies, stews and other home-made dishes. Haydn sometimes brings some of them down to mine when he comes to visit as he says his dad can't eat all of this on his own. It's lush though my mum thinks it's great and she loves Haydn like another son. She was so worried about him when he had his transplant and thought he wouldn't make it at one stage. I know my dad didn't want me to keep seeing him as he thought I'd get terribly hurt if anything happened to him. Now that he's stabilised and his medication is sorted they are much happier about me being with him. I know they actually love him to bits.'

They walked out into the early afternoon sunshine. People were starting to arrive and were mingling around looking at the stalls and chatting. There were plenty of children and there was a queue already forming waiting to have a ride on one of the two ponies that Vicky Butler had brought along from the nearby stables with one of her stable girls. Vicky had inherited a farm with stables and livery yard from her parents and had made it into a very profitable business. Posy had never had much to do with horses but went over and patted one of the friendly, little ponies. She said hello to Vicky who seemed interested as to who she was.

'I've heard you're staying at the house tonight. Have you known Tim long?' she asked inquisitively.

'Not very long, no. I'm just here for the night. It seems a lovely village. How did you know that I was staying?'

Vicky raised her eyebrows and said, 'Well, this is a small village and news travels fast. There are all sorts of rumours going round. Some true, some not, who knows.' She shrugged and with that she had to see to another small person who wanted a ride on one of her ponies.

She'd be one to watch if you lived around here, thought Posy. She's quite the village nosy parker and I'm sure there are a few of those in the neighbourhood. It's a small community and there's bound to be gossip and a hierarchy between the residents.

The fête was starting to become busy with all sorts of people arriving in their bright, summer clothes. Luckily, it was a beautiful day and not the disastrous wet English Summer Bank Holiday afternoon it could have been as in some previous years. Last year apparently it had rained all afternoon despite being August and had been a complete washout.

A number of the parishioners she met seemed great characters if slightly bizarre. As she walked around she saw that there was a long table with vegetables neatly laid out. This was the best organically grown vegetable competition. Some of the entries were rather wonky but there were some tremendous marrows, pumpkins and one of the largest cucumbers she had ever seen. They were all neatly labelled with the grower's names. She stopped to chat to the lady behind the table, who introduced herself as Maisie Appleton, she informed Posy that the Vicar was due to judge the vegetables at 4.30. Things were getting very tense with the other competitors apparently but she was sure her husband would win for his cucumber this year. He had been cultivating it with great care all summer and it had grown to the large size that she saw before her fed with purely organic material. Posy made a mental note to go back there at 4.30. She'd love to see who won this. So parochial, such an example of English country life, so Tim, maybe.

She met Mrs Wilson, of coffee and walnut cake fame. She was running the cake stall with her daughter and they were doing a flourishing trade with locals and tourists alike wanting to sample and buy her lemon drizzle and fruit cake laden with brandy-soaked raisins.

She met Mr Harvey, the Church Warden, who had been helping out as such for many years, long before Tim had arrived as Vicar and had seen to three other incumbents before him. Posy suspected he must be in his eighties but was still sprightly and obviously very together mentally. She remembered some of the residents at the care home that she looked after who were not so fortunate. Dementia had robbed them of their identities and caused devastating effects on their families who sadly they sometimes never even recognised.

'You know there are 40 weddings booked in for this year,' Mr Harvey told her proudly, 'most of them will have confetti and I'll sweep up every last piece of it. I love it, it adds something special to the atmosphere. These days it comes in all sorts of shapes: stars, leaves, butterflies, hearts you name it. Some churches ban it but not us. Now rice, I don't like that and it hurts when it hits you. I can't understand it. Biodegradable my foot.' Posy smiled, she told him it had been lovely to meet him and moved swiftly on.

Her eye was caught next by a woman who she imagined must have been in her 50s. She had long, blonde tresses, undoubtedly with some help from hair extensions and she had very black, fake eyelashes. She was wearing a short skirt and as she swept past Posy there was a haze of strong, not very pleasant perfume. She has a slightly orange tinge and looks a bit too done up, thought Posy, and then rather unkindly, 'mutton dressed as lamb.'

Chloe who had wandered off to talk to someone else was now beside her and she noticed Posy's gaze.

'That's Henrietta Harker no man is safe from her or her cronies. Haydn told me about her, poor Tim had to fight her off but I think she's got the message now. She's been married three times and on the look out for a fourth poor victim.'

There were several other women of a certain age who seemed to be congregating together and Posy observed that these were probably the village clique. They would in all likelihood make it their business to know everything that was going on in their area.

After she'd spent some time at the fête, bought a few little trinkets to boost the church funds and had a cup of tea and a piece of cake from Mrs Wilson's stand, Posy decided to take a walk around the village. She'd enjoyed walking as a pastime since she was a child and her parents would take her all over the country to find interesting walks and most of their holidays had revolved around this activity. She'd taken Josh for long rambles across the countryside too when he was younger and they had gone on a couple of walking holidays together but then he had started wanting to go away with his friends, understandably. Latterly, she had been on several walking holidays with a group of like-minded people and they'd visited places in the United Kingdom as far afield as Cornwall, Scotland and the Lake District. They would stay in quaint little hotels or guest houses en route. Sometimes they'd have someone to drive their luggage from one stop to the next so they didn't have to worry about carrying their bags; she was on holiday after all!

Whilst walking she found it a good time to think and put the world to rights. She'd met some interesting people who she had made friends with and arranged to meet up with again. They were usually people of similar tastes who had a mutual love of nature and enjoyed observing the beauty of the countryside and all the natural world had to offer. She had met some people to be avoided though who were extremely boring and she had had to march on ahead with some excuse.

Bolingbroke was an extremely pretty, little village with its Cotswold stone honey-coloured cottages and their pale green front doors. As yet unspoilt by large developments and housing estates. The roses climbing around the doors and windows making it a typical picture book village and jigsaw puzzle favourite photo. With this attribute it attracted day trippers which greatly boosted the takings at the village shop and also the contributions in the church donation box.

The small river which flowed through the village was a tributary of the Thames. How strange that this was a link to London. It seemed a different world away from the capital city and the connection to the river there. A duck paddled past with her downy ducklings following, their small, webbed feet furiously paddling behind her whilst she dipped and dived for tasty morsels below the water. This has to be one of the most picturesque villages in the country, thought Posy, it's just beautiful and so quintessentially English. I can see why Tim loves it here.

She passed some rather grand looking gates. There was a notice that said rather threateningly;

'Bolingbroke Manor, Strictly Private, Tradesmen's entrance to the right'

Well that could be interesting I'd like to walk up there, she thought. I don't want to trespass but I'd love to see what the house looks like. She walked past the tradesmen's entrance and tried to peer through the gates but it was such a long drive with numerous big hydrangea bushes in flower and large, billowing oak trees that she couldn't even catch a glimpse of the house itself. This left her even more curious as to what the manor looked like and who lived there.

Next, she came to the pub. She knew that they were going there for a drink and a bite to eat that evening so she had a look at the menu outside. Typical pub grub but that'll do me she thought I could eat most of the things on that menu. It looked very welcoming and there were a number of people inside already and even more sitting outside in the garden area with dogs of all shapes and sizes basking in the late August, pleasingly hot sunshine. The village was a renowned beauty spot and she was aware that there were many tourists and sightseers who would visit to enjoy the photogenic beauty of the region. She had noted that many of the visitors at the fête were probably not locals either. They were having a day out in the country and lapping up the atmosphere. It was all good for business if they were spending their money in the pub and helping to boost the church funds.

When she arrived back at Church House the stalls and gazebos were in the process of being taken down and there was a great tidying up exercise going on. She'd been so engrossed on her walk that she'd forgotten the time and missed the vegetable judging. Mr Harvey was dealing with the litter and muttering to himself about the mess that had been left.

'Surely not locals, it's all these day trippers who come in and can't be bothered to put their rubbish in the bin.'

Posy went up to her room to freshen up. She could hear the telephone in the hall downstairs frantically ringing then stop and start ringing again. Someone on the other end was being very persistent in wanting to be answered. She never could bear to leave phones unanswered, no doubt something ingrained from working in the care home and the difference that a phone call could make to someone's life. She proceeded to go downstairs intending to answer it and to write a message for whoever it was meant for. At that moment, Tim came in through the front door and picked up the phone, he gave her a wave of acknowledgement and she heard him exclaim and say, 'I'll be right round.'

He turned to Posy, gave her an exasperated look and said he was sorry but he had to go out. There was a bit of a problem with a couple of the villagers who did not see eye to eye. He hoped he wouldn't be long but as it was getting late why didn't she go along to the pub and he'd join her there after he'd sorted out this little problem.

'Tell Debbie, the landlady, to save a table for us please. Haydn and Chloe are joining us there too.' And with that he dashed off.

She knew that he was the vicar but wasn't sure all that this position entailed. She had only met him a few times and she was a guest in his house but it seemed to her as though he was clearly at the beck and call, or felt duty bound, to his parishioners' needs and wants. She changed into her dress and walked down to the pub which was buzzing with a great atmosphere.

Haydn and Chloe came into the pub and

were greeted by Debbie who showed them over to the table where Posy was already sitting. Shortly afterwards Tim came in, saying he could do with a strong drink, he'd just had to split up a fight between Ted Appleton and Mick Hughes. It was Maisie Appleton who had been on the telephone begging the vicar to come round to their house straight away. Mick had turned up in a terrible temper accusing Ted of cheating with his giant cucumber that had won the best vegetable prize. The produce in the competition was all meant to be completely organic. Mick was determined that Ted's wasn't and he'd gone round to Ted's garden shed and found a bottle of chemical fertilizer which he knew that he'd used and which was strictly against the rules.

Mick also accused Ted of apparently tipping a whole load of snails over his garden wall under the cover of darkness and they had played havoc with his lettuces and chewed holes all over them. 'I knew it was him that done it, who else would want to do that?' he asked of Tim accusingly.

'Honestly, you couldn't make it up. Ted had rolled up his sleeves to punch his accuser.' Tim explained that, in the end, he had managed to smooth things over between the two men and persuaded them to shake hands and resolve their differences. It appeared that there was a regular disagreement that happened every year between the two old gardeners about something or other. They had both lived in the village all their lives and gone to school together. It had been a lifelong love/hate relationship apparently but then they would meet up in the pub over a few ciders and become best of friends again, until the next spat.

Tim eventually started to relax after his refereeing and the four of them enjoyed their meal with a good few drinks to wash it down with.

That evening Posy climbed into the sunken, old bed. It was strangely comfortable despite its seemingly lack of springs. Her head was buzzing with everything she had encountered over the day. She could sense that Tim was a very popular vicar but also that there was some tension there about him with some of the residents - Vicky, for example - but she shrugged it off. She kept thinking of Tim's smile and the people she had met at the fête and in the pub. She had so enjoyed meeting

Chloe, and of course, being with Haydn.

She missed the fact that her own son would never have a girlfriend and that she wouldn't have the opportunity to have a daughter-in-law and the potential for grandchildren. She had a sense of a foreshortened future, which she knew was possibly an avoidance symptom of post-traumatic stress following a bereavement but she knew that it was a fact that she could never possibly have grandchildren now. Josh had been her only child and all hope of grandchildren had been taken away from her with his death. She tried to divert her thoughts with some meditation and mindfulness that she'd learnt and eventually had one of the best night's sleep she'd had for ages.

CHAPTER TEN

Posy kept herself busy, work was frantic and there were a great many new rules and regulations being brought in which meant that she had numerous statutory training programmes to go to. She now had so many certificates that it took up a whole separate file in her work folder.

Her day at the care home started early. She'd go in and have a meeting with the care assistants, then she would assess which patients needed specialist nursing care that day. She loved the job but found it sad that most of the residents had been sent there by their family or doctors because they could no longer look after themselves. She had a special bond with Mrs Laney but she also enjoyed talking to the other residents. People like Edith who was 92; she had delightful recollections of her time as a teenage shop assistant in an upmarket stocking shop in Knightsbridge, London.

'Once I travelled up in the lift with the Queen of Holland. She had two bodyguards with her and I thought, cor, they look nice. We had a lot of royalty coming in.' Recounted Edith.

Posy loved the wisdom of life and tales of another era that the residents told. Their names were from the past, names like Ethel, Alfred, Dot, Winifred, Gladys, perhaps those names would become fashionable again but for now they seemed dated, of their time. They talked about jobs they had that no longer existed (switchboard operator, draper, tobacconist, ironmonger).

Posy was dismayed by the number of residents who only had occasional visits from their family. She knew that they would go back home tomorrow if they could but there was no chance for that now their houses had been sold to pay the care home fees. Posy reflected that ageing is a natural thing but fundamentally hard, that is if you're lucky enough to get old.

She'd go round to Angharad and Jeff's for dinner and other friends would be there. Sometimes they would try and set her up with a date but she wasn't interested. She went out with her walking group and would spend time in her garden when the weather was good.

Posy also kept in touch with Haydn and over the next couple of months she'd visited Bolingbroke a few more times. Haydn had suggested she visit when Chloe was there, and this was a good idea as it helped to have someone else around almost to act as an intermediary. She wanted to see Haydn and know he was doing well but was sensitive to the fact that she had to be careful not be too intrusive or clingy. She understood that she was very privileged to have such a good rapport with him and his family but he had his own life and was getting on with it which was excellent.

Whenever she contacted Tim he was usually busy with his jobs and he would take ages to answer her text or email. If he wasn't preaching or writing a sermon, he was visiting the housebound or his sick parishioners in hospital. When she visited Church House, the telephone always seemed to be ringing with parishioners in crisis or someone fundraising or wanting to organise a wedding, christening or funeral. Tim certainly had a busy life tending to his flock but he did manage to make time for her on her visits and was always very attentive and charming.

She enjoyed her visits to the village and her walks around it and each time she visited she was gradually getting to meet some more of the locals and knowing her way around. One night when they went in to the pub for a glass of wine before dinner she asked Tim who lived in the Manor House.

'Clive Cameron-Clarke lives there with his wife. He is not a pleasant person. I don't have much to do with him if I can help it.' Tim hastily replied and it was left at that leaving Posy slightly mystified.

Then her attention was drawn away as she thought she overheard someone say, 'That's Reverend Tim's girlfriend' and she looked over to see two ladies who averted their eyes when they saw her looking at them. They were obviously talking about her and Tim.

Is that what I am she questioned to herself. I think I certainly have become a friend to Tim and I enjoy his company but nothing to suggest that he has any feelings for me apart from the link that we have between our sons. The village tittle-tattle was evidently starting.

She had prepared a casserole at home and brought it with her to heat up that evening and an apple crumble with the cooking apples that had blown off the tree that morning.

As Posy had cooked the meal and Chloe had helped lay the table the men decided, amicably that they thought it was 'right and proper' that they cleared away and did the washing up. Their offer was duly taken up and soon there was a clatter of plates and glasses being washed and placed on the drainer and good-natured banter and laughter coming from the kitchen. Chloe and Posy sat back in their chairs, poured another glass of wine each and chatted to each other smiling at the noise coming from the kitchen.

'Tim really likes you, you know,' said Chloe.

'Do you think so? I thought he just felt a bit compassionate towards me what with me losing Josh and Haydn benefiting from it, so to speak.'

'Well I've known Tim for three years now and he's never had anyone else that he's spent so much time with. I know he's had a few problems with a couple of ladies in the Parish chasing after him. Henrietta for a start and then there was another woman who really had a crush on him. It was so obvious, she just kept popping round with all sorts of lame excuses just to see him. He just wasn't interested and she started to be rather a pest.

She was married as well. I think in the end, Tim had to speak to Mandy, the counsellor lady who had a quiet word with her and she stopped coming round after that,' she said rolling her eyes.

'Well, I really like him too,' said Posy and then felt that maybe she shouldn't say too much to the younger woman about her feelings for Tim. They had drunk a fair amount of wine that evening and she didn't want to say anything she might regret later. She was rather encouraged by Chloe's remark though.

Chloe told Posy how she had met Haydn at the agricultural college where they were both studying. It was an instant attraction between them both and they had been together pretty much since then. She had been doing landscape design and the garden at Church House had been one of her projects for her degree, so she had been up there with Haydn to stay most weekends for at least six months

'It was a great garden for me to practice on as I had complete free rein and I gained a really good degree for my project work. Of course, it was always a worry with Haydn's health and he couldn't do anything for a few months after his operation as he had to take it easy but we've been together through all of this. I've started my own business now and it's really taken off. Haydn's going to come into the business with me. My ambition is to show at the Chelsea Flower Show one year; that would be amazing.'

It was obvious from what she was saying that she was deeply in love with Haydn and it was heart-warming to see her so inspired about their life ahead. She must have felt, at one stage, that he possibly wouldn't have a long enough life to be able to plan for the future.

CHAPTER ELEVEN

Birthdays and anniversaries of important personal dates are the hardest days to bear when you are bereaved. The run-up to these dates can actually be far worse than when the actual day arrives. So many memories of your loved one and what you had celebrated with them in previous years. The heartbreak of not being able to share the occasion with them again in the future.

It was coming up to December and Josh's birthday, it would be the first without him and she was dreading it. She tried not to think too hard about previous years but she remembered how he so looked forward to it. The planning what he was going to do, who to invite, the cake - even as a teenager he still wanted Posy to make a celebration cake for him with candles. Last year he'd had two cakes. She'd managed to find a 1 and a 9 shaped cake tins and made a nineteenth birthday cake for him complete with nineteen candles. Posy had organised a traditional birthday tea for him with his favourite childhood treats and put balloons and decorations around the house. Twelve of his friends had come round and then he had gone off to the pub with them to celebrate. She thought they'd probably gone on to a club afterwards as Josh hadn't appeared from his room until the afternoon the next day. He came downstairs nursing a very sore head and looking rather rough. He didn't elaborate on how the previous evening had gone but it obviously involved rather a lot of alcohol.

The date of Josh's birthday came. Angharad phoned, as did Tim and plenty of her friends remembering what the day was. After four telephone calls she just couldn't talk any more so unplugged the house phone and closed down her mobile, she took a mild sleeping pill and was in bed by 8.30. Sleep is bliss for helping cut out those thoughts that she just couldn't bear to think about any more. The pain of missing him was like a hurt that would never heal. Worse than anything she had felt in her life.

I would give anything to have him back. I'd have cancer, I'd give my own life to have him here with me now but you couldn't bargain with life like that and fate had its own destination.

There were times when she'd be out, walking down a street and catch sight of a young man and think it was Josh. This happened many times. Her logical mind knew that it wasn't him but a hope, just a hope that maybe it was all some sort of terrible nightmare and she would wake up and life would be back to how it was before the accident.

One time when she turned and looked back at a Josh lookalike he looked at her and smiled. I hope he doesn't think I'm some kind of weirdo woman ogling him but if I told him why he made my head turn it might unsettle him. You had to be careful, some people found loss difficult to talk about. Couldn't face it. Stupid really as death is all part of this rich pattern of life but humans like order and the natural order of things is not for your children to die before you.

She got through the first birthday without him, but then, oh God, what was she going to do about Christmas? That would be a big thing to deal with. Everyone seemingly being happy and spending time with their families, it only rubbed salt into the wound of loss and sadness.

Both Haydn and Tim had asked her if she would like to join them and their extended family at Bolingbroke for the festivities, but could she really join in with this new family that she had been brought together with by such unusual circumstances? His parents were coming, she knew they were in their late seventies but apparently in good fettle. His sister, Susan, would be there with her husband and their two teenage children and Samantha's brother would also be there with his wife and their youngest child and, of course, Haydn and Chloe would be there too. Quite a crowd, and she just didn't know if she could cope with meeting them all for the first time, cope with her grief and celebrate Christmas, when for her there was nothing to celebrate. She counted up the people - thirteen. Oh well, that's an omen then, she thought, we can't have thirteen around the table, especially at a vicar's table. She laughed at her silly superstitions. She knew that Tim wasn't superstitious but wasn't that why the number thirteen was unlucky because Judas who betrayed Christ was the thirteenth person to sit down at the Last Supper?

I'll have to make up my mind soon.

Angharad who she had spent many a Christmas with in the past was having to go back to Wales to see an aged uncle who in all probability wouldn't live to see another one. So that left her with three choices. Do I stay at home and have a miserable Christmas or do I go and celebrate with the residents at the Care Home or do I go to Tim's and meet all his family? When she put it to herself this way it seemed the only sensible thing to do would be to go to Bolingbroke for Christmas. She phoned Tim to let him know her decision and to ask what she could bring and what about presents for all his family?

'Oh please don't bring any presents for me or my family. Christmas gets ridiculous, it's far too commercialised these days, besides which you've never met them so I wouldn't expect you to bring presents for all that lot.'

She felt a sense of relief at having made the choice to go, and also at not having to buy presents for people she had never met before. As soon as she had put down the phone she put her coat on and went into town with the prime purpose of shopping for a new dress, shoes, and to buy a present for Tim. I'm going to buy one for him she thought even if he doesn't get one for me. I think he's a lovely man who has been through a difficult time. He has a busy job and from what I can gather he has no one in his life to make a fuss of him and he deserves it.

Christmas Eve arrived and she packed up her car for the couple of nights she was going to spend at Church House. It was a busy time of the year for Tim and she knew that he would be out working for most of it but she'd be there for him when he came back to the house and she had to admit she was excited at meeting his family. She was very pleased with the new outfit she had bought and it made her feel pretty and special. She had bought Tim a Merino wool jumper in a dark green colour. She was sure it was just the sort of thing he would like. She'd really splashed out and it was a good quality one. She'd noticed that his clothes, although probably very expensive when first bought were now starting to look rather frayed around the edges. I bet he hasn't been shopping for clothes since Sam died, she thought.

Posy arrived at Church House and rang the doorbell. She was beginning to feel like a regular visitor but that was just it, still a visitor. A refined looking older lady came to the door. She was very upright, and sprightly and Posy guessed that she was in her late seventies and also guessed, correctly, that this must be Tim's mother. She was wearing a beautiful silk dress with a matching cardigan, very elegant and she immediately felt a bit self-conscious arriving here like this with her overnight bag in one hand and a bottle of champagne in the other. His mother would know all that was going on in her family and know who she was and that her son had been the heart donor for her grandson.

'Ah come in my dear, you must be Posy and I'm so pleased to meet you. Come in and meet all the crew.'

As Posy entered the house there was a pleasing, homely smell of something roasting mingled with baking coming from the direction of the kitchen. She put down her overnight bag and handed Mrs Woburn Smith the bottle of Champagne she had brought. She then remembered the mince pies she had made the night before were still in the boot of her car. In total this year she had made 60 mince pies. She always made some for the residents and staff at the care home and she'd brought 20 with her today. She rushed outside and collected them. Handing them over to Mrs Woburn Smith she said 'I hope that'll be enough, I know there are going to be rather a lot of us.'

There was a large Christmas tree in the hall and boxes of decorations were littering the hallway with shiny baubles and tinsel falling out of them. Two teenage girls were sitting on the floor going through the boxes and giggling over how gaudy the old decorations were. 'Oh look at this one, Lydia. I really think Uncle Tim needs to get some better decorations for Christmas these look so tacky! Mum, Mum, can we go into the town and get some more decorations these look awful,' cried Francesca.

Two golden retrievers bounded into the hall, jumping on the boxes and adding to the chaos. 'Get down Mungo, Jerry come here,' ordered the woman who was trying to subdue them. She introduced herself to Posy as Susan, Tim's sister.

'No, you'll have to make the best of what's here. There'll be nothing in the village, there's only one little shop and that's got nothing in it and I'm not going all the way to Oxford on Christmas Eve, it'll be chaos. Let's have a look and we'll see what we can do.'

Posy went upstairs and quickly dumped her bag in her usual bedroom. Tim had already told her that he'd reserved that room for her. It was going to be a full house but he wanted her to be comfortable and feel at home.

She went downstairs and got to work looking through the assorted cardboard boxes with Susan, Lydia and Francesca. They were all laughing and joking about how awful all the old decorations were. After much hilarity and differences of opinion about where the various decorations should be placed the Christmas tree looked very pretty with baubles everywhere and silver and gold tinsel hanging from it. Three sets of mini lights, with lots of bulbs unfortunately not working, were wound around from the top to the bottom and a battered fairy had been stuck right at the very top. They all thought it looked great if a little bizarre and haphazard.

'Now we can start putting the presents underneath then it'll really look like Christmas,' said Lydia.

***

On Christmas Eve Tim conducted a Christingle service at 2.00pm, family carols at 4.00pm and midnight mass at 11.00pm. Then, on Christmas Day he took the Holy

Communion service at 9.00am and the family service at 10.30am and also made visits to Parishioners who needed both his spiritual and his worldly guidance on this special day for the Christian community. Sometimes, Tim felt a slight annoyance that people who didn't visit church from one month to the next visited at Christmas and in times of personal difficulty. This was human nature and he knew that he was there to help whoever chose to come along and make their peace with God, or the Supreme Being, as they knew and needed it.

Posy had been to the family service with the rest of the Woburn Smith's. Tim stood there in his white and gold robe, which he'd explained to her, was worn at Christmas and Easter to symbolise the birth and resurrection of Christ. To her he looked resplendent and as he conducted the service Posy admired his confidence and felt a surge of happiness that she hadn't felt for months. It was then she realised that she liked him more than just a friend but that she was falling in love with him. The way he held the congregation's attention and the obvious respect that his parishioners had for him made her feel proud of him.

The two teenage girls had taken some persuading to join them but in the end had reluctantly attended. Once the hymns and carols started they were competing as to who could sing the loudest and trying not to collapse into giggles when the organist played the wrong notes. Both were in the choir at school so were more than happy to join in with that part of the service. As for Posy, she wasn't particularly religious but she enjoyed feeling part of the family and also feeling integrated into the village community. She listened intently as Tim gave his sermon and Christmas message that she knew he had been working on for ages. She felt it was poignant and atmospheric; he was a charismatic speaker. She felt annoyance at Lydia and Francesca as they were messing about, pulling faces and pinching each other in the pew in front of her. Susan seemingly oblivious or beyond care as to her daughters' behaviour.

Christmas lunch time arrived and eventually Tim came back to the house. He looked tired but perked up after a glass of Champagne and proceeded to be the perfect host. Making sure all his family were happy and being fed and watered well. He wasn't a big one on presents as he'd already warned her and had bought a job lot of chocolates, albeit expensive ones, and that was what everyone received from him, including Posy.

Samantha's brother Gordon and his wife, Marion, arrived later than expected. The family were into their third bottle of bubbly by this stage and were getting rather worried about the vegetables being cooked to pulp when the doorbell rang and there they were. It wasn't a long drive for them but they seemed rather stressed when they arrived and piled into the hallway with bottles of wine and laden with presents. They'd driven from the Midlands for lunch along with one of their three children, Jane.

'This is the first year we haven't all been together, I've been trying to phone the boys all morning and they're not answering their phones. I mean it's Christmas Day they've got to speak to their mother,' said Marion who was obviously very irritated that their two eldest children had chosen to be with their girlfriend's families.

Susan had laid an extra place and placed a teddy bear on a chair to make it fourteen. 'We can't have thirteen around the table, I'm much too superstitious,' she exclaimed. Posy decided that she liked Susan and they had a long conversation mostly about Susan's yoga lessons. They did touch upon her and Tim's childhood briefly and his obsession with sport, particularly rugby. She asked Posy if she had met any of Tim's friend's and in particular, Mark. Posy replied that she hadn't yet as she didn't get to see Haydn and Tim that much.

'Oh okay, I just wondered how often Tim got to see Mark now,' and she gave Posy a wary look which left her feeling slightly puzzled.

Christmas lunch was cooked by Tim's mother who as matriarch of the household made it her place to take charge of the family meal with help interspersed from Susan and Posy. The delicious smell Posy had noticed when she'd arrived on Christmas Eve had been the turkey cooking. She always cooked it the night before she said.

Marion wasn't in to cooking by her own admission. 'I gave it up a long time ago. Sad but true. They've all survived somehow.' She laughed. Posy wondered whether this might be why her boys would rather be elsewhere.

Tim said Grace before everyone sat down. 'Dominum Nostrum,' he started off; 'Oh for God's sake Tim,' said his father, 'at least you could do it in a language that we all understand. Latin is a dead language.'

'Father, please,' Tim gave his father a dirty look mixed with a smile of amusement. 'It's Christmas and I only say Grace in Latin once a year as you well know, so "vos sedatos esse".' This was obviously a private joke between father and son and Tim went on with the Grace but she noticed sniggers from the girls present and Haydn gave Posy a little smile.

That was something that Posy found difficult to get used to. Tim would always say Grace before a meal, although not usually in Latin as he started to today and also not at breakfast, thank goodness, she thought. Well I suppose he is a vicar and that's what they do. It was all good-natured banter from his father though, but his mother bowed her head and looked serious.

The wine flowed and ostensibly it was a happy celebration, but who knew what thoughts were buried in the minds of those present? She didn't know the family dynamic, having only just met them. There were always skeletons in the cupboard and secrets in families that lurked beneath the surface.

Just after the Christmas pudding had been

doused with warmed brandy, set fire to and brought flaming to the table, Tim gave a little speech and thanked everyone for making it such a lovely day. Posy felt moved to tears when he made a special reference to her and to Joshua for enabling Haydn to have his heart transplant and acknowledging how hard it must be for her today. Haydn reiterated that point too and as she wiped away a tear Mrs Woburn Smith reached out to her and squeezed her hand, she gave her a sincere look of sympathy that Posy appreciated and sensed was heartfelt.

Shortly after this when Posy had regained her composure and glasses were refilled Haydn clinked on his wine glass.

'Ladies and gentlemen, Chloe and I have an announcement to make. We're going to get married.' He pulled Chloe from her seat and picked up her left hand, 'You're an unobservant lot. She's had this ring on all day and nobody has noticed. I've already done the old-fashioned thing and asked her parents for her hand in marriage. Thankfully, they agreed and are really pleased so we hope you all are too.'

Chloe blushed and looked at Haydn with a clear look of love in her eyes. 'I think we knew we were right for each other as soon as we met,' she heard Chloe saying to Susan, 'but Haydn was unsure of his future health wise and wanted to wait until he'd had the all clear from the cardiac team which he now has.'

She showed the family her pretty pink sapphire and diamond engagement ring. It was so unusual in its design and resembled a rose with tiny diamonds encrusted in the white gold around the open petals either side of the pink stone. There were more celebrations and rather a lot of champagne was drunk.

Once everyone had moved away from the table and washing up and general debris had been tidied away they all settled down in the sitting room to watch the usual stuff that was on the TV at Christmas. All of them, apart from the three teenage girls who had better things to do or watch upstairs away from the boring confines of their family. The three girl cousins got on well and after lunch they all went up to listen to music or phone friends on their mobiles or whatever else they felt was more riveting than sitting around with their parents.

Festivities were brought to an end suddenly

for Tim and he'd had to sober up pretty quickly as a distraught parishioner came knocking at the door having had an argument with his wife and wanting to see the vicar. It sounded as though there had been a terrible drama at the house and things had become violent so he'd taken refuge and come to see the vicar.

'That's the problem with being a vicar,' said Robert Woburn Smith. 'It happens every year some bloody person having too much to drink and arguing, buggering up his Christmas. All the tensions of the year seem to come to a head at Christmas and Tim has to deal with it. Still that's what he signed up for. Don't know why he couldn't have been an accountant like me.' He had been Chief Accountant at a large, private company and had done very well out of it and invested well. Robert wasn't particularly religious and often said he didn't know where Tim had got all his godliness from. He had been an ambitious father and encouraged the children with their school assignments and didn't take failure well. Each parent gave them different aspects to life and through their parents' differing ideas Tim and Susan had benefited and been happy and fulfilled children.

It was Lillian, Mrs Woburn Smith, who had looked after their children's spiritual education. She was the one who had taken them to church on Sunday and tried to instil in them kindness and Christian values. She had been interested in many other religions and was well read and open-minded. It was for this reason that she believed Tim had gone into teaching and then decided to turn to God and take holy orders. Susan had always been a thoughtful, spiritual child too. She now was a yoga teacher also interested in meditation and mindfulness. She had a great following as a yoga teacher in her leafy London suburb where the beautiful mummies and ladies who lunched had no qualms in paying her increasingly pricey sessions. One of the rooms in their large Victorian detached house boasted an ashram and there she would balance the chakras and troubled minds of stressed and overworked, ambitious professionals stressed out by life in the fast lane of corporate life. Susan had married an accountant, however, which had pleased her father greatly and also boosted the family income and allowed them an affluent lifestyle.

The life of a vicar, however, is not affluent and Tim had given up a good income as a headmaster to fulfil his spiritual path. Yes, the house and help with upkeep was a perk of the job but it was nothing like the comforts and quietude described by the likes of Jane Austen in her novels. In reality the job was hard work and stressful with constant calls and interruptions on his time, so to be a really earnest parish priest one had to be absolutely dedicated, which Tim surely was.

Tim was nearly an hour in his study helping the overwrought man calm down. Eventually, the voices from the study stopped and Tim showed the now much calmer man to the front door. Posy heard the sound of Tim's footsteps across the hall and him talking carefully to the man. She overheard Tim offering to give him a bed for the night if he needed to return that evening. He never ceased to amaze her with his dedication. The front door eventually closed and she heard him going back into his study and closing the door. The rest of the family had retired to their rooms and Posy decided it was time for her to go to bed as well. She went to say goodnight to Tim in his study where she found him beginning to look at one of the books he had been given as a Christmas present. He put the book down as she entered the room and looked at her with a weary smile.

'It's been such an amazing day; I've enjoyed it so much. I know you've still had to work through it all though. You must be exhausted so I'll leave you to wind down but I just wanted to say that I love your family and it's such fantastic news about Haydn and Chloe.'

'I know, I'm very happy about it. They are a good team together. It's such a miraculous relief as this time last year we didn't know if he would be able to continue with his work and now here he is with a new heart and planning to get married. And I've met you.' He smiled at her and Posy noticed that he looked worn out and had tears in his eyes. This strong man who had always been there for everybody else, a pillar of society and there for the most important highs and lows of his parishioners' lives. He was generous in his goodness and in giving of his time, and she knew that he needed someone to support him and look after his well-being too.

She didn't know if it was all the wine that she had consumed over the day but somehow it felt just right to lean over and kiss him. He seemed surprised for a split second but then his mouth was over hers and she was surprised by his reaction as he responded by kissing her back fervently and passionately. He took her in his arms and held her close to him. 'I've been wanting to do that for ages,' he said. 'Just our luck that we have a houseful tonight but I want you so much.'

Posy went to bed and thought about the kiss with Tim. So, Chloe had been right in her observations and she realised that there definitely was something that was blossoming between them. How strange, she thought, that we should meet in the way we have. She imagined what it would be like to sleep with him and hold him through the night and to have a full relationship with him, a proper sexual relationship. It had been a long time since she had felt anything romantic towards a man and she definitely felt a sexual frisson for Tim. Who would have thought that I'd fall for a vicar, the idea made her smile. I'm not sure I can take all his work pressures though it certainly is a lifestyle choice and not just a career. And I used to think they only worked on Sundays and did weddings. How wrong I was! She settled into her lumpy but comfortable bed, smiled a contented smile and fell asleep.

CHAPTER TWELVE

After Christmas things definitely stepped up a notch in Tim and Posy's relationship and they talked frequently on the phone and e-mailed regularly. They would talk about what was going on in their lives generally and laugh about amusing things that had happened at work or with the people they encountered. They were comfortable in each others company and their friendship was growing. There was more between them than just the unique bond which their sons shared that had initially drawn them together.

Tim was so busy in the parish with his ecclesiastical work and then there was the charity that he supported and the rugby team which he helped train. This meant he rarely had any time off which made it difficult to have any meaningful time together. The vicarage might have been a family home for Tim but to the parishioners, the down-on-their-luck, random passers-by and the plain nosy a parish vicar's house is a public space with the activities of its inhabitants a fascinating contribution to the rolling drama of parish life. Like the Vicar of Dibley but for real.

There were plenty of purposeful parish ladies who wanted to help the poor man living on his own with his son who had been so ill. There were always people turning up needing advice or just a talk with the vicar. Too many prying eyes were aware of the fact that here was a good looking, widowed vicar and there was an attractive lady who came to visit occasionally so they had to be discreet and private about their burgeoning relationship if they didn't want it to become village gossip. There were already rumours going around about the Vicar's 'lady friend' - who was she and how did he meet her, they wanted to know?

One night when they were having a long conversation over the phone. Tim said that he desperately wanted to see her.

'I know, I want to see you too. I can't bear all this sneaking around that we have to do and I know that Chloe is so busy with work that she's not coming up to Bolingbroke for quite a while. What can we do that isn't going to get all the gossips going?' pleaded Posy

That's when they decided to meet up at a hotel for a couple of nights. It would be a good getaway for both of them. It couldn't be a weekend as this was just too busy a time for a vicar. Tim said that he'd have a look on the internet and find somewhere they could meet up. Somewhere far enough away from their own homes where they couldn't, hopefully, be spotted by anyone they knew and where they could just enjoy being with each other.

'It'll be a relief to get away completely,' said Tim. 'What about Wales? I don't think we would run into anyone we know there. I haven't had a break for years and the last time I went away it was camping in Cornwall with the Scouts and it rained every day. One of the little cherubs broke his leg falling out of a tree and I spent most of the time running him about and talking to his hysterical parents and trying to calm the other kids down. It was not a success as a holiday on my part.'

Posy felt a thrill of excitement every time she thought about spending a few nights away with Tim on their own. They would have a double room she knew. They had both had other partners and knew what to expect. It wasn't as though they were in the first flush of youth and had never been in relationships before.

Tim booked everything and planned his getaway carefully by making good excuses. Posy caught a train to their destination and Tim collected her at the station in his battered old Volvo. When he'd been in teaching and Sam had been alive they would buy a new car every other year, but he'd taken a dramatic drop in salary on becoming a vicar and couldn't afford to do that now. He didn't care though; as long as it got him from one place to another; that was the important thing.

When Posy arrived at the station she excitedly disembarked the train and made her way out through the exit. There was his car, he was waiting for her. As soon as he spotted her he jumped out of the car and picked up her bag and put it in the boot. She reached out to him and gave him a quick peck on the cheek. It felt slightly uncomfortable and self-conscious, but also exciting knowing that they would be alone in each other's company for two whole nights. They chatted about her journey on the train and his drive down and commented on the wonderful Welsh mountains in the distance as they looked out of the window and at the countryside around them. They joked about the amount of sheep there appeared to be as soon as you crossed the border into Wales.

'I've already checked in,' said Tim, 'it's a beautiful hotel, I think you'll like it. It's so great to get away and have you with me. I feel like a teenager again.'

Tim certainly had chosen well. The hotel was nestled in the heart of the Welsh countryside and offered a perfect blend of classic country charm mixed with luxurious modern details. They went up to their room and Posy gasped as she took in the magnificent four poster bed and stunning views from the enormous windows of the surrounding rolling hills and the Black Mountains in the distance. Before she had a moment to take it all in Tim took her in his arms and kissed her passionately.

'I have been waiting for this moment so long. It's been unbearable having you near me and not being able to show you what I feel for you.'

He took no time in gently pushing her on to the bed and kissing her lips, her cheeks and her neck. Posy was absolutely ready for this. It had been a long time for both of them since they had any passion in their lives.

'No, wait,' said Tim suddenly retracting, 'I want this moment to last. You know I want to make love to you but I want to wait until after dinner. We've waited this long, let's savour the moment.'

Posy did not want to wait; she wanted Tim right there and now. She loved him and fancied him passionately; just the thought of having sex with him made her heart beat faster. She had been thinking of it all through the train journey, imagining how he would be. The feel of him caressing her. They had kissed before which had been wonderful but there had never been the right time for love making with all the intrusions of every day life.

'No, I don't want to wait, I can't, come here,' she pulled him towards her and felt for his belt buckle which she started to undo. She could feel that he was sexually aroused and despite his protestations she brought him to a stage where he could not refuse her.

'We can do it now and again later,' she gently teased him.

Their lovemaking was exquisite, he was a gentle lover and seemed to know the right places to touch and at the right moment. Posy felt so right making love with him and a tingle of excitement ran through her at the thought of Tim inside her. Tim, the sexy vicar. Tim, her lover.

They lazily regained their composure and Tim got up to have a shower. Afterwards, he went down to the bar and said he'd meet her there once she'd got ready.

Posy had a bath and smiled to herself at what had just happened between them. The sex had certainly lived up to her expectations. It could have been stressful being with a new partner but with Tim it just felt right and she hoped that he felt the same about her. She put on the new dress that she'd bought specifically for the occasion and felt she looked pretty good in it. She'd had her hair done, which admittedly was a bit rumpled now, but she fluffed it up and applied some make up. She hadn't had a tryst in a hotel bedroom for years, plus with a man she was falling in love with made it doubly exciting so this was certainly an occasion for her.

When she went downstairs to the bar Tim was obviously impressed with the way she looked and paid her lovely compliments about her dress and hair. He told her she looked beautiful and she certainly felt glowing. Dinner was probably very good but they weren't paying too much attention to the food and as they gazed at each other over the table Tim opened up to her a bit more.

'You must realise that I have strong feelings for you Posy. I loved Sam, we had a good marriage, we were young and had, so I thought our future before us but with you it's different.'

'What, you can't see a future with us?'

'No, that's just it. I don't know if it's because I'm older now but I feel differently about you. This is something else, I really feel that I've known you all my life; with you I feel as though I've found someone who is on the same level as me.'

After they'd finished their meal and had a liqueur - brandy for him, crème de menthe for her - they went for a short walk in the hotel garden. It was still early in the year and the night was chilly. Tim took off his jacket and placed it around her shoulders. If it didn't seem such a cliché, she would have said that it was a perfect moonlit night; and then he kissed her. She remembered their lovemaking before and couldn't wait to repeat it over and over again. Her passion left unfulfilled from years on her own was coming out. She loved the feeling of wanting to make love, to be close to someone again, it made her feel alive.

Tim couldn't believe how fortunate he had been in meeting Posy. He hadn't thought he could have another relationship with a woman and now she had come along. He was starting to feel that he loved her and that night he showed her how much and told her that he loved her.

Throughout the night Posy glanced over at Tim, watching him asleep, the curve of his cheek and his masculine smell. She smiled and felt happier than she ever remembered with a man.

What she didn't know was that when she wasn't looking at him, he had awoken and looked over at her. He felt blessed that he had found such an amazing woman. He had been lonely and he was enjoying having someone beside him at night. He needed her in his life and he wanted to assure her of his feelings by making love to her again.

The next day they slowly woke up and listened to the birds singing outside their window. It was cold outside but they dressed up. Tim had told her to bring her walking boots, he knew how much she loved walking. He'd arranged a picnic with the hotel and off they went walking in the breath-taking Brecon

Beacons. They climbed the highest peak, stopping at the summit to admire the fantastic views. They were lucky that despite the time of year and although cold it was a clear day and from the top they could see right over to the Bristol Channel and even towards Exmoor in Devon. Tim spread his coat out and they sat down to eat their very welcome picnic. The climb had given them a ravenous appetite. The walk took them three hours and by the time they got back to the hotel they were exhausted.

The next morning Posy woke up and stretched over to Tim. It had been the most amazing couple of nights and she felt surprisingly and dizzily in love. She knew that Tim felt the same by what he had said and his actions towards her. She didn't want to go home to her empty house and the mundane every day routine of work and household chores. She wanted to stay with him and in his arms forever, feeling the solace in her body in the touch of someone else's skin. She had no idea what the future would hold but they had Haydn and Chloe's wedding to look forward to and she was taking life one step at a time. She had learnt that one never knew what life might throw at you and to seize the day was her new motto.

CHAPTER THIRTEEN

The date had been set for Haydn and Chloe's wedding 'We're giving you the day off dad,' said Haydn. 'Chloe wants to get married from her parents' house so we're having the wedding in Devon. As it's March the weather probably won't be too good so we've opted for the reception at a hotel rather than a marquee in her parent's garden. Her folks really wanted us to wait until the summer but we've waited so long, what with me being ill, that we didn't want to waste any more time. Also, the summer is hectically busy for Chloe with the gardening business and I'm going to be joining her in the venture too so we just won't have any time off at all during the summer'.

Invitations were sent out, Vicar and venue booked, food and wine chosen. The next thing and most importantly for Chloe were the flowers and of course, the dress.

'I'm having my dress made, I've decided,'

Chloe told Posy, one weekend when they were both at Bolingbroke. 'I just don't like anything I've seen in the shops or online. My mother's friend is a dressmaker and I've described exactly what I want and she's taken my measurements and she's making it for me. I'm going to buy the bridesmaid's dresses though. There are four of them so we just wouldn't have the time to make all of them.'

She showed Posy a sketch of her dress. It was a very elegant sheath dress with a train, long lace sleeves and a boat neckline.

'White, of course. I hardly ever wear dresses as I don't get much chance to in my line of work; so I'm really going to enjoy dressing up for the wedding and the going away outfit.'

'What shoes are you going to wear?'

'I don't know. I haven't decided on that yet, I've been too busy with the dress and flowers but yes, I guess that is a very important part of the outfit.'

Posy had an idea. 'What about Samantha's shoes in the spare bedroom? I'm not sure what size they are but we could have a look. I think it would be lovely to wear something that belonged to your mother-in-law on your wedding day even though you never met her.

I'm sure Haydn would find it very touching; it would be like having a bit of his mother's memory present. He will be upset, of course, that his mother isn't there to share his special day. You might even find a dress that you could use for your going away outfit as well as some shoes. I know the clothes are small and might not be to your taste but you can't be more than a size 8 yourself and retro is very fashionable. What comes around goes around, especially in fashion.'

'Yes, I think that's a lovely idea; let's go and have a look. I keep meaning to ask Haydn if he knows all her things are in the spare bedroom. I don't think that he does and I guess they can't stay there forever.'

They went up the stairs with excitement to have a look through the treasure trove of dresses, shoes and handbags in the wardrobe.

As Posy was staying in the spare bedroom and her things were in there anyway she opened the door and showed Chloe in. She was beginning to feel like it was her room although she knew it was only temporarily hers as a visitor.

This was all for show of course, the bedroom wasn't too far away from Tim's and tiptoes in the night and furtive couplings had been happening since their tryst at the hotel. Tim was aware of prying eyes, however, who might want to know the finer details of the vicar's sleeping arrangements with his lady friend. He wanted to try and keep it as clandestine as he could which was kind of exciting but frustrating for her and she wanted to shout about their love for each other and the happiness she felt.

Chloe rushed towards the wardrobe with excitement and flung the door open.

'I knew these things were here but like you didn't want to intrude before,' she said. Now, however, they did intrude but they didn't feel awkward about looking through the clothes of the vicar's late wife as neither had ever met her and somehow it didn't seem too personal to them.

'I wonder what she was really like,' said Chloe. 'Haydn doesn't talk about his mother much. I don't know if it's because he finds it upsetting but I've asked him about her a few times and he just clams up. I know she was fairly delicate with her heart problem and couldn't do too much. I get the impression she was rather wrapped up in cotton wool and Tim did most of the hard work. I think it was difficult for him working so hard, having a sick wife and a young son who wasn't in good health either.'

'I know,' said Posy, 'I've tried a couple of times to talk to him about her but he just doesn't seem to want to, so I don't mention her at all now. I think he was devastated when she died and it's just too painful a memory for him.'

They pulled out a few of the dresses and there were several that Chloe loved. She selected a classic tea dress in a very pretty Liberty print. She tried it on and it fitted her perfectly.

'That's the badger,' exclaimed Chloe.

'What?' Laughed Posy.

'Oh that's a West Country saying my family use when we've found something exactly what we were looking for. That's what my mum said when I met Haydn. That's my pet nickname for him 'Badger'. I think it's quite sweet and it suits him.'

'Well, yes, you look absolutely beautiful in that, you should wear that as your going away outfit. It could be a little chilly being March though. I wonder if there's a jacket or coat in there that might match it.' They had a look through and found a short wool navy blue jacket that matched the navy in the dress and would keep her warm.

'Now what about shoes?' said Posy. She rummaged around one of the shelves and through the shoe boxes. 'These all seem to be a 5, what size are you?'

'Perfect, I'm a 4 ½ to a 5 so they should fit depending on the make. Let's have a look.'

They pulled out several of the boxes and had them scattered around the floor. They were enjoying themselves like two children let loose in a sweetie shop, exclaiming over the lovely shoes.

'These are so pretty I've never seen anything like them before,' said Chloe. She had found a pair of pale blue satin shoes with diamanté buckles that were exquisite. She tried them on and they fitted perfectly. They decided together that she had to wear those with her wedding dress.

'Something old, something new, something borrowed, something blue, that sorts out three of the four traditions in one item,' said Posy.

Chloe opened another of the shoe boxes that was at the very bottom of the wardrobe. It had been covered over by a tangle of silk scarves.

'What's in this one? It feels pretty heavy.' She opened the lid and there inside were what seemed like a bundle of letters.

'What have you found there?' asked Posy, looking over to Chloe with intrigue.

'It's a load of letters. They look like love letters, oh my goodness, I don't think we should look any more; they're too private. I think they're letters from Tim to Samantha, probably from when they were going out together, before they were married. Hang on. No, this one says *Darling Sam* and ends *I love you. Yours forever Alan,* and look at the date at the top, it's dated only a year before Sam died.' She flicked through the pile of letters quickly.

'They all seem to be to Sam from this Alan person. Oh wait a minute, there is one here from a solicitor in Oxford, Roberts, Asher and Stephens. It seems to be talking about divorce proceedings.' She looked shocked and quickly put the letter back in the box.

They both agreed that these were very personal and none of their business so Posy bundled them up and put them away again.

'This just doesn't feel right,' said Posy. 'Let's take the things that you want to borrow, put them in your bedroom and go downstairs. We'll have to leave all this for another day. I feel quite shocked. Poor Tim. It's obvious that

Sam was having an affair and even thinking about divorce right up until she died. I'm sure we'd find out more if we read the letters but it's not the right thing to do. It's in the past and it should stay in the past. Do you think Tim and Haydn knew about this?'

Posy looked up and saw that Haydn had come quietly into the room. He just stood there looking at them both with an angry expression on his face and he was absolutely silent. She felt as though she had been caught red-handed, like when she was caught eating chocolate by her mother at Lent or when she had been smoking and blowing the smoke out of the window at the nurses' home and matron had come in and castigated her only the way an old fashioned matron could. A tingling feeling of conscience came over her She looked over at Chloe guiltily and the three of them said nothing for several seconds.

Haydn was the first one to speak.

'Are you enjoying yourselves rifling through my mother's things?' He said scathingly. He had an aggravated look about him and Chloe had never heard him speak in that tone of voice before. Posy, who did not know him so well, imagined that it must be the emotion of seeing his mother's possessions laid out in front of him. Perhaps it was bringing back long-lost feelings and he couldn't deal with that.

'Oh Haydn,' said Chloe, 'we knew some of your mother's things were here and I wanted to surprise you at the wedding and wear something of hers. You're not angry are you?'

'We'll have to sort all these things out sometime, I'll speak to Dad about it.' Said Haydn and stormed off.

Posy and Chloe looked at each other their feelings of elation and excitement for the forthcoming wedding preparations dampened by Haydn's reaction to them going through his mother's possessions. They hastily tidied up the room with Chloe taking the favoured dress and shoes to her shared room with Haydn and then they both eventually met again downstairs in the sitting room.

'I don't know what's got into him,' Chloe said, 'I think maybe all the wedding plans have got too much for him. To be honest he didn't want a church wedding at all he fancied just going to a registry office and getting it over and done with as quickly as possible. He's had enough of church life as he feels it's been rammed into him all his life and I don't think he even believes in God or all that malarkey. He knew that I wanted the big, white wedding though, and so did my mum, so he's just going along with it. Maybe that's why he's got the hump. I'll have a little word with him later and try to calm him down.'

There was a definite atmosphere at dinner with Haydn saying very little and not having any eye contact with either Posy or Chloe. Once or twice Chloe's eyes met Posy's and she raised them skywards, as if to say 'typical man.' Posy felt uncomfortable with the situation but she noticed that Tim was his same usual self and seemingly hadn't picked up on the chilly atmosphere.

***

Haydn had known about his mother's affair. Several times when he'd been home in the holidays he'd met the man who seemed to turn up at the house regularly while his father was away. Perhaps just a coincidence he thought at first, but he wasn't stupid and recognised the growing friendship between his mother and Alan. He'd read the body language when he saw them shift quickly apart in the kitchen when he'd walked in one morning to make a coffee. There was another occasion when he'd heard his mother talking quietly on her phone with a soft voice and thought he could make out 'love you too'. At first he thought it was his father she was talking to but then realised that it wasn't when his father phoned shortly afterwards and her tone of voice was completely different.

Even though he had suspected his mother of having an affair, he hadn't known about the letters in the shoe box and this had shocked him when he'd found out. He had overheard the girls when they had discovered them and he knew that they would be from the man he now hated. The man he knew had been his mother's lover and made her betray his father. It brought back so many feelings that he didn't understand and couldn't control.

He'd loved his mother, of course he had, and partly he blamed his father for never being around and always too busy helping out other people. He knew about his father's temper, but even though he was quick to flare up, it usually subsided pretty quickly and then he would be his usual happy dad again. The school teacher, sportsman and later the vicar that everyone found to be a thoroughly decent chap.

His father had left the transfer of furniture

and other contents in the house to the removal men who'd literally just packed up the old house and brought it to Church House. He had been too deep in his grief and too immersed in his new tenure to be involved in household duties.

Later that evening when Haydn and Chloe had gone to the pub, Posy felt the time was right to bring up the subject of the clothes in the wardrobe. She wouldn't mention the discovery of the love letters and felt if he was unaware of them then it was best left unmentioned.

She told Tim about the clothes in the wardrobe and, like Chloe had suspected, he had no idea that they were there.

'I just never go into any of the other rooms upstairs to be honest. Old Mrs Chiltern sorts out all the laundry and makes the beds up if we have visitors and I'm not interested in any of that, never have been. Well, we'd better take them to the charity shop. Do you want any of them?'

Posy laughed, 'Tim, you must remember what Sam was like and look at me, I'm two sizes larger than she was. They are lovely clothes and thank you for the offer, but they definitely would not fit me and they wouldn't be Chloe's sort of thing either, although the shoes are her size and I think she would love them.'

It was agreed between them that the clothes would be bundled up between her and Chloe at a later date and taken to one of the charity shops in the nearby town. Chloe would be bequeathed the shoes as they were her size. Posy felt a sense of relief that a mutual decision had been made. It was a sensitive subject and not her remit to decide what happened to his deceased wife's clothes, but now that she had been given permission she felt it was fine to dispose of them and clear the wardrobe.

CHAPTER FOURTEEN

The day of Haydn and Chloe's wedding
came, family and friends congregated in
Devon for the celebrations. It was March so
the weather was chilly, but it didn't rain
which was a blessing.

As they all filed into the church Posy felt a
surge of emotion but also rather
uncomfortable. She'd bought a new dress for
the occasion and she knew it was rather tight.

'It's a bodycon dress,' the shop assistant
had said. 'It's meant to be figure hugging and
it looks wonderful on you. It just feels strange
to you as you've never worn one before but
you'll get used to it.'

Well she wasn't getting used to it and she
realised she had made a big mistake. She'd
bought the dress at Araminta's, an expensive
ladies dress shop in Beaconsfield, it was on
the sale rail at a bargain price that was too
good to miss. She had loved the royal blue
colour as she felt it brought out the blue of her

eyes. It had long sleeves and came to just above the knee. She had squeezed into the size 12.

'Are you sure it's a size 12, it looks more like an 8?' Posy had asked, feeling very vulnerable in her lack of fashion judgement, but relying heavily on the opinion of the assistant. She had phoned Angharad at that time who had encouraged her and said she had a couple of bodycon dresses and she would get used to it.

'I love it though and I want it so much.' So that was how she ended up with the beautiful but unbearably uncomfortable bodycon dress which she now promised herself she would never, ever wear again and would be going on ebay as soon as she possibly could with all proceeds going towards her charity. She had fully been intending to lose half a stone before the wedding. Although she'd tried not eating for a couple of days and cutting out bread and potatoes for weeks beforehand it was still too tight. She breathed in her tummy and hoped she'd be able to get through the day without bursting the seams. How on earth am I going to be able to eat anything at the reception, she panicked.

She was seated on the side of the

bridegroom with Tim and his family. The pale sun had peeked out from behind the clouds and was making a welcome brightness to the already happy occasion.

Crashing rolls of organ music announced the arrival of the bride. Above her head Posy heard the church bells ringing out joyously. As Chloe walked down the aisle there was a gasp of appreciation from the guests. She walked proudly on the arm of her father as the wedding party began to move at a regal pace. She looked radiant in her beautiful, sheath-style, white wedding dress which fitted her perfectly and showed off her slender figure. All those fittings had certainly paid off especially as she had lost half a stone in the last three weeks, and hasty, last-minute alterations had to be made. The dress was elegantly plain, the boat neckline showing off her lovely neck and the long sleeves trimmed with lace and coming down into a loop that slipped over her finger and gave the sleeves a long, graceful line. There were small crystals dotted over the bodice and she had a long veil held in place with a crystal tiara. She carried a small bouquet which was made by one of her garden designer friends who had grown the flowers especially for the occasion. As it was spring she had daffodils and freesias, interspersed with forget-me-nots and grape hyacinths. The yellow of the daffodils and blue of the other flowers looked striking.

Two tiny bridesmaids who were her sister's children followed her and behind them were two of her best friends who helped look after the little ones as they started to get fractious and pull flowers from their bouquets which were in little wicker baskets.

Beneath the hem of her wedding dress peaked the blue satin shoes with diamanté buckles that had belonged to her late mother in law.

Haydn turned around to look at his bride as she was walking down the aisle. He made a funny face most likely through nerves, but it was the sort of thing that Josh would have done. She'd noticed a couple of times mannerisms that Haydn had adopted which seemed familiar. She wondered if she was imagining the likeness or had the heart imparted some of Josh's characteristics onto Haydn. She told herself she was just being sensitive; it was an emotional time after all.

Posy wiped a tear from her eye at the sentiment of the occasion and glanced at Tim who also had a slight tear in his eye. He gently rubbed her hand in support. It was such a poignant yet painful day for Posy seeing the young man who now had her son's heart becoming a married man, hopefully continuing on to a long and successful marriage and career.

The reception was held in a hotel in Budleigh Salterton, it was slightly shabby and could have done with refurbishment, but the food was good and staff were pleasant. Posy and Tim had booked a room there and as soon as the speeches were done and it was reasonably polite to leave the table Posy went up to their room to change into another more comfortable outfit.

Later in the evening the music started and most of the guests sparked into action and had a turn on the dance floor. When Tina Turner's Simply the Best started up, Tim took her hand and guided her up to join the others flailing around trying their best to keep time to the music. By this stage she'd had quite a bit to drink and was feeling very relaxed, also thankful that she'd changed into something more comfortable. Tim whispered 'you're simply the best' into her ear and picked her up and spun her round. She felt dizzy and was laughing so much she had to steady herself by placing her hands on Tim's shoulders. She spotted Susan watching them with a curious look on her face.

Later whilst Posy was dancing with Tim's father, Posy looked over and noticed Susan talking animatedly to Tim. She glanced over to Posy and gave her a small wave and quickly diverted her look. Posy had the feeling they were talking about her, but maybe she was imagining it.

When they wandered up to their bedroom, weary and slightly tipsy after all the festivities, Posy fell giggling onto the bed and pulled Tim towards her. She placed one of his hands between her thighs and with her other hand she started unbuttoning his belt and reached for his zip. He looked at her earnestly, took her in his arms then flopped down onto his back.

'I'm sorry,' he groaned, 'I think I've had too much to drink,' and he fell asleep snoring after seconds. Posy was disappointed. This was only the second time they had managed to get away together and she had been so looking forward to being in his arms and holding him close to her. Their past sexual activity had been good but not that frequent, however she was just pleased to be with him and she felt sure she loved him. With Tim she felt safe and secure. She told herself that not every man wants sex every night and it had been a long day.

There had been evenings when she had been at Church House when they had curled up together in their nightclothes, not bothering to try. He liked to cuddle her though and she was happy to be in his company. He told her how lovely she was, and kissed her on the mouth but after that it didn't really gel the way she would have wanted it to. It was disappointing as things had started out well on the sexual side. She would have to think how to approach the subject in a sensitive and sympathetic way when the time was right.

The next morning after breakfast, still hung over, they went out for a drive. They needed some fresh sea air to blow the cobwebs away and they decided to visit Exmouth, and although chilly it was sunny and they huddled up in their winter coats and scarves and walked along the promenade, looking out over the two miles of sandy beach. They walked along holding hands and as they came to an octagonal shaped kiosk Tim let go of her hand and went to the kiosk. She looked out over the beach drinking in the beautiful vista and breathing in the cold, salty air. She had never appreciated the sea much before, usually preferring country views, but she was spellbound by the constant movement of the sea and the people enjoying the beach.

Posy intently watched a man and small boy with a dog, throwing a ball over and over for the dog to retrieve. The dog never seeming to get bored with repeating the same caper tirelessly and wagging its tail joyfully. Tim came back with two enormous cones filled with smooth tasting, whippy vanilla ice cream.

'I know we're cold enough already but I just fancied one and couldn't resist,' he said smilingly, handing one to her and taking an appreciative lick of his own.

'I haven't felt like this for years; I feel like a child again.' He winked at her and her heart reached out to him.

When they had nearly finished eating their ice creams and were crunching the cones with their faces turned towards the sea admiring the view, Tim suddenly turned to her.

'I don't know if I've said it before but I love you, Posy White. I know this might come out of the blue to you but I've been thinking of nothing else since I met you. Would you like to become a vicar's wife?' asked Tim.

Posy looked at him incredulously. This was not something she had been expecting. She hadn't seriously thought about them being together as a couple, full time, forever. She thought he was too involved with his work and other interests. Yes, she loved being with him and he was the best thing that had happened to her in years, but a proposal that was another thing. The thought had crossed her mind whether she was in love with Tim because of the connection between their sons or if she truly loved him. That was a conundrum that played across her mind. She didn't want to have those doubts and once again wanted to 'live in the moment.'

'Is that a proposal?' she asked.

'Well yes it is. Actually, I mean, will you marry me, please?' He dropped down on one knee in a dramatic, mock proposal.

'I'll say it again, Rosalind White will you marry me?'

Although his proposal came as rather a shock to her she knew that he sincerely meant it and must have been mulling over the idea for a while. Tim was not the sort of person who would do something as major as this on a whim. It was the best thing, at that time, that could happen to her, apart from Josh being resurrected that is, and she knew that could never happen. She quickly made a decision that she couldn't refuse his offer.

'Oh Tim, of course I want to marry you. Yes, yes, yes.'

He kissed her passionately there and then in full view of the other walkers along the promenade, neither of them caring who saw, both completely happy with their decision and knowing that they would now be able to show their love openly in the parish if they were engaged. It formalised things, and although Tim was very open minded, he'd had to be exemplary in his life as a headmaster and then a vicar. Some members of the congregation were still rather old-fashioned. He wanted to keep his respectability in the Parish and if he was married he felt that would give him more credibility. He didn't want to upset the parishioners.

He had a secret though and one day when the time was right he would tell Posy about it but it had to be delicately managed.

'You've made my life complete. I never thought I could feel happy again after losing Josh, nothing can replace him and I think of him everyday. Having you and Haydn and meeting all your family have helped to heal things so much. We've both had some hard times and as we've learnt to our cost, life can be terribly cruel. I think now that my motto is "seize the day" and right now I'm going to,' said Posy.

'Ah yes, Carpe Diem,' said Tim. I think we owe it to ourselves to take some happiness whilst we can.'

She was a bit concerned about the way he had said 'Would you like to become a vicar's wife?' she thought no, I don't want to be a vicar's wife I want to be *your* wife and she felt she had to mention this.

'Tim, you know I'm not particularly religious and I don't think I can be a dutiful vicar's wife. Of course, I'll support you in the Parish and as much as I can with fund raising and things, but I still want to have my own career, it's very important to me.'

Tim took this on board and agreed she would find a job nearer to him. It was exciting discussing and planning their future lives together. Posy would sell her house and move in with Tim and find a job so they could be together all the time.

'We'll tell my family about our engagement

tonight but try and keep it relatively quiet until I tell the Bishop which I'll do as soon as we get back. I don't want news to break out in the village too soon.'

'When we're ready I'll tell Nancy Wagstaffe in confidence and then in next to no time everyone will know,' joked Tim. 'There will be gossip aplenty mark my words, they will love it. Then, my darling, the next thing is going out and buying you an engagement ring.'

***

Tim was right. Just one mention to the village gossip and the whole Parish was abuzz with the rumour about the vicar marrying his lady friend, although they had made sure the reason of how they had met was a well-kept secret.

'I told you so, didn't I?' said Nancy Wagstaffe, the Parish Secretary, to Mrs Wilson. 'I could tell the first time I met her and I thought then, oh this is the vicar's new girlfriend. It's about time he remarried, he's been a widower for too long. Men have wants and needs you know, even the vicar,' she had a smug, all-knowing smile on her face. She liked to know everything that was going on in her village and prided herself on the fact that she knew about most things first.

'Yes, she does seem like a very pleasant person. It's a shame his first wife died at such a young age and he's had all that time on his own with a sick boy to look after, so good for him that's what I say.'

Next time they visited The Lion, as they went through the door, most of the locals turned around and gave them a cheer. Debbie said. 'We've all heard the news, this calls for a celebration,' and off she went to the fridge and brought out a bottle of bubbly. She proceeded to open it with a large pop and poured the happy couple a sparkling glass each and for anyone else who wanted one. With the Champagne flowing well, Edward Wagstaffe, Nancy's husband, shouted out to Debbie

'Another one on me.'

When that bottle had been emptied Henrietta Harker bought another one. Posy noticed rather unkindly that Henrietta had applied far too much lipstick which was rapidly being transferred to glasses and whatever cheeks she could reach. Tim was trying to rub away a bright red ring that she'd managed to plant on his cheek by way of congratulations.

They all wanted to see the ring which Posy proudly showed them to lots of exclamations and 'Ooh's and Aah's.' Henrietta seemed very happy for them, but underneath she was slightly jealous that she wasn't the lady announcing her engagement to the fit, rugby playing vicar. There was quite a party going on and everyone was getting tipsy and rather loud. An engagement no matter how old the participants are is a great way to put a smile on other people's faces and theirs was no exception.

Generally, the Parish were delighted. He had a fiancée and would shortly be marrying her. There was also a rumour that she was starting a new job at the doctor's surgery as a practice nurse.

This, in fact, was not a rumour. She had no problem with her nursing experience in finding a job as a practice nurse at the surgery a few miles away in another village. It was just the sort of job she had always wanted.

Posy had wasted no time in giving in her notice at the care home. She firstly told Mrs Laney about her engagement and proudly showed her the pretty ring to prove it. Mrs

Laney was delighted.

'Well my dear, I'm so glad you are happy. Make the most of it while you're still young and just go ahead and enjoy yourselves. Old age is no fun I can tell you but I'm very glad that I had a jolly time while I could,' she said with a gleam in her eye.

Posy looked down at her pretty emerald and diamond engagement ring. They had chosen it together in a jewellers in Oxford and it suited her very well. She hadn't wanted anything flashy, that was not her style. It was very pretty though, just three small emeralds set in yellow gold surrounded by diamonds. Tim had really pushed the boat out and she felt so spoilt, she had never owned anything like it before

CHAPTER FIFTEEN

Miranda Cameron-Clarke was blonde and beautiful, she turned heads wherever she went with her statuesque, model looks and confident air. She looked amazing in her tight jodhpurs and knee high riding boots. She was more interested in her horses than she was of her husband, Clive. She had given up with him a long time ago and as long as he continued to pay the bills and let her buy more horses she would stay with him. She also had a fairly successful business herself but she knew she could fall back on her husband's finances if she didn't have any commissions for a while. That was partly the reason why she had married him. He had the right contacts for her business but since they'd moved to the country her horses were her main enjoyment and work had paled into insignificance in importance to her.

'I don't care how many women he shags now, in fact I wish he would go off with one of them then I'd have the house to myself,' said Miranda caustically.

'I know, I wish Pete would find someone. No one would have him though with his disgusting habits and lack of personal hygiene,' said Vicky,

Vicky had met Pete at school, was impregnated by him at 17, married and had four children in quick succession. All before the two of them were 24. She had been running her father's stables and livery yard very successfully since then and had some of the best horses in the county being stabled there. She worked hard while Pete hung around pretending to see to general maintenance but was more often found chatting to the owners and smoking with the stable hands rather than doing any useful work. Their children all still lived at the farm including ten-year-old twins from their firstborn.

The two women had become great friends and shared their common love of horses, travelling around the country to equestrian events with their horse boxes in tandem. They'd not long ago attended the Cheltenham Festival at the invitation of one of Clive's business colleagues. The adrenaline had been running high and this man's horse, Major Caramel, had won the hurdle race. Afterwards, they had gone into the owners' enclosure where they'd met the horse's trainer and Miranda was enthusing about him and how gorgeous he was. She was angling at an invitation so she could meet up with him again, trying to find a reasonable excuse to visit his stables and, contrive to accidentally, on purpose, bump in to him. The two friends were plotting the best way to do this. Miranda was nothing if not ambitious and if she wanted something she usually achieved it.

Often, when they'd finished their ride and put their horses away they would arrange to meet up at the Lion for a drink or have a light lunch there, which is what they had decided to do on the day Posy first encountered Miranda. She thought she'd surprise Tim and take him out for a meal so she'd gone in to the pub to book a table for dinner in the evening.

As she walked in to the Lion, and as most of the lunchtime trade had left, she noticed the two ladies sitting at a table by the window finishing off their lunch. They seemed rather an incongruous pair. The one born and bred as a country girl to the life of looking after horses and, the other, being brought up in

London as a City girl but wishing to be a country girl all her life. Despite their different upbringings they were as thick as thieves and were obviously good friends and confidantes, their love of horses and contempt for their spouses bringing them together in convivial friendship.

The two women looked over at her, and as Vicky realised that she recognised her from the fête, she shouted out 'Hello.' Posy thought she overheard her say 'that's the vicar's bit,' in a stage whisper and she felt self-conscious. She didn't like the way they made her feel but knew that this was a small village and everyone would be interested in what was going on, especially if it involved a person so central in its daily life as the local vicar. She found herself smiling in a forced way and saying 'Hello' to Vicky anyway.

'Have you met Miranda?' Vicky asked.

'No, I haven't.'

'Miranda lives at the Manor with her husband, Clive.'

'Miranda, this is Posy, she's engaged to the Vicar.'

Miranda's eyebrows lifted, 'oh really' she said, 'that's interesting. Please join us, take a seat, I'll get you a drink. What would you like?'

Posy noticed that they were both drinking white wine so she said that would be lovely and she'd join them in a glass of the same which Miranda duly bought for her.

They continued chatting and Posy told her how she'd walked past the gates to the Manor several times and was intrigued to know what the Manor was like and especially the gardens. She told them that she loved gardening and would be very interested to see the gardens there as she could imagine they were wonderful.

'The gardens aren't so wonderful at this time of year I'm afraid, but you're very welcome to pop round sometime and I'll show you around the house. Why don't you come round for coffee one morning. What are you doing tomorrow? Come round about 11.00 and I'll be there. Would love to show you around. We've done some amazing things with the house, totally updated it. I'm an interior designer you know.' Posy said that she'd love to visit and made a mental note - 11.00 tomorrow morning.

Miranda finished her white wine with one final gulp and stood up putting on her riding jacket ready to leave.

'Got to go now, bye, see you tomorrow Posy. Cheers Vicky, see you Thursday for our usual ride out.' And with that she was off leaving Posy at the table with Vicky.

Now that Posy was left alone with Vicky she felt slightly uncomfortable. She wasn't used to drinking in the afternoon and the wine was going to her head. Vicky had insisted on buying her another. She knew that Vicky was a local born and bred and she was a newcomer and even though Tim wasn't originally from the village, he was their vicar and she felt a bit of an interloper. Vicky proceeded to tell Posy about the Cameron-Clarkes. How Miranda had been something in the interior design world in London and had met Clive who was an amazing and very successful architect. He'd designed many notable buildings in London. She must know about the innovative mushroom building that he'd built which was such a contemporary building that had won awards for its design. After his recognition for that he'd been contacted by a scout for Sheikh Rashid Bin Makhtoum and was granted a commission in Dubai to help with the development of a four-star hotel and also a residential tower. This had made him a good deal of money and because of his connections with the Sheikh and his reputation as a brilliant architect he was well sought after and at the height of his career.

Vicky seemed rather star-struck it appeared to Posy, while she had no interest in the lives of the Cameron-Clarkes other than that they lived in Bolingbroke and she was interested in their house purely from an aesthetic point of view.

Posy looked forward to the morning and going to have coffee with Miranda. She wondered if her husband would be at the house. She was curious to meet him, he sounded an interesting character.

***

Posy hadn't had a chance to talk to Tim about her invitation for coffee at the manor. He had been tired when he'd come back from his ministrations for the day and had set off early that morning to conduct matins.

It was only a short walk to the gates of the manor but the driveway must have been about half a mile long through parkland. The drive was an avenue lined with oak trees that must have been there for hundreds of years, their giant boughs billowing out and looking majestic. The oaks had iron cages around them presumably to stop deer from gnawing at the bark and damaging them. Interspersed between the trees were large hydrangea bushes. It seemed to take her ages to get to the house but she enjoyed the walk and it gave her an opportunity to enjoy the scenery and grounds.

As she walked further along the drive the parkland turned to formal gardens and then suddenly she saw the house, appearing impressively before her.

The manor house wasn't as big as she was expecting but it was certainly very pretty, built from soft honey-coloured Cotswold sandstone. It had three gables and was completely symmetrical with a large wooden front door exactly in the middle. Large mullioned windows were set decoratively within the stone.

She approached the impressive, wooden front door and rang the door bell and heard deep chimes from inside. She waited a while and then the door was opened by a man. She reckoned he was probably in his mid-fifties, of medium build, pleasantly featured with smooth black hair and brown eyes that were almost black. His skin was slightly sallow and his legs were rather thin but overall he was decent looking in a rather dissipated way. He looked as though he smoked and drank a bit too much. He had a deep, well-spoken voice with a received pronunciation accent. He was wearing corduroys with a tweed jacket and she suspected he would favour chinos and an expensive polo shirt in the summer. She thought he was the type who had probably never worn a pair of jeans in his life and certainly would never, ever, ever wear a T shirt, or God forbid have a tattoo.

'Well hello, lovely lady, I don't think we've met before, I'm Clive Cameron-Clarke and who are you?' he said to her in a charming but slightly over-confident manner.

'I'm Posy White, I met your wife yesterday and she invited me round for coffee this morning.'

'Oh did she? Well, I'm afraid she's not here right now, left in a bit of a hurry. She'll probably be back at any minute. Don't know where she's gone. I expect she's just gone out to see to the horses; they take over her life those damn horses. Come in anyway and you can make yourself at home while you're waiting.'

She entered the hall which was elegantly furnished. There was a large hall table with a big silver dish and a huge display of fabulous roses and calla lilies, their scent permeating the whole room. Above the hall table hung a large picture of highland cattle and there were other oil paintings that looked like very expensive originals which took up most of the wall space in the hallway.

As they went through into what Clive called the 'snug', which was anything but snug, she noticed that it was decorated in a contemporary style but had maintained its original features. All the furnishings and decorations were either white or gold which although quite dramatic, to her taste she felt were rather colourless and overly ostentatious.

She exclaimed as she walked in and Clive turned and smiled at her, obviously pleased with the impression that the house had made on her.

'We had a lot of work done here before we moved in and then Miranda added her magic touches. The bathrooms were in a terrible state and we completely gutted the kitchen and added on a conservatory. So how did you meet Miranda and have you lived in Bolingbroke long?'

Posy explained that she had met Miranda yesterday in the pub and that she didn't live in Bolingbroke, she lived in Buckinghamshire but she was engaged to Tim Woburn Smith, the vicar. She thought she saw Clive's countenance change when she mentioned Tim but maybe it was imagined. She had felt overly sensitive since Josh's death and knew that sometimes her feelings had been all over the place and maybe her judgement wasn't as good as it used to be.

He walked over to a silver tray which held an array of very expensive looking decanters holding all different colours of drinks, he gestured at her: 'Fancy a drink?'

She said that it was rather too early in the day for her to start drinking. However, despite the early hour, he poured himself what she thought, judging by the colour, was a large whisky.

Suddenly she felt vulnerable and no longer wanted to be there, in a strange house with this rather charming and evidently successful but slightly unusual man.

Where was Miranda? She had invited her for coffee and now she wasn't at home. She couldn't have forgotten since yesterday surely.

Clive came and stood very close to her, too close, she could smell the whisky on his breath. He was drunk she realised. God, it was only eleven in the morning. Had he been drinking at breakfast?

'Well, well, so vicar Tim has got himself a fiancée. So how is the schoolmaster priest?'

Posy didn't like the tone of Clive's voice and drew away, looking out of the window and hoping Miranda would come in at any moment. She decided to make her excuses and leave. She scribbled out her name and mobile number and handed it to Clive asking him to pass it on to his wife.

Clive went on, casually taking a long sip of his whisky, 'I had dealings with Woburn Smith years ago. My son was at a school where he was the headmaster. Didn't like the man. Messed my son's schooling up completely. His wife died suddenly, you know. Strange business that. She'd been having an affair with a father of one of the pupils at the school, a good friend of mine. Odd how she suddenly died like that. Maybe he murdered her in anger when he found out he'd been cheated on,' he said nastily and then he lurched towards her.

She didn't like this situation. Definitely

didn't like it at all. Then when she felt his hand on the top of her leg, she thought it was a mistake and that he had just brushed past her too closely. When his eyes wandered down to her breasts and he looked at her lasciviously that was just too much.

'My eyes are up here!' she said sarcastically.

'Don't be so timid, you're a grown woman and so very pretty too. Doesn't that vicar fiancée of yours give you any pleasure? Or maybe he's not interested in women. I have my suspicions.'

Posy could feel the fear and anger building up inside her. This sort of thing had not happened to her since she'd been a teenager when one of her father's respected and trusted friends had chased her round the dining table trying to kiss her whilst her parents were out of the house.

She was furious at his lewd advances and accusations against Tim. She summoned up all her strength and gave him a straight punch with her right fist. She'd had a few Taekwondo classes with Josh at one stage and now she was grateful that the training had come in handy.

Clive keeled back, put his hand to his face

and looked completely shocked.

'What did you do that for. I didn't mean to upset you,' he said with a shaking voice.

'Don't you ever mess with me again or talk about Tim like that. I mean it.'

Clive looked absolutely stunned. He had definitely met his match with Posy and he realised that he had made a gross mistake. She wasn't the easy touch he thought she might be, but a feisty woman who was not impressed by him or by anything that he might have. She could take him on at his own game.

She wasn't going to let him get away with his behaviour. He was right, she was a grown woman and she could deal with someone like him. She stormed out of the house. Her heart was beating so fast but she had to smile to herself. I think I handled that pretty well, she thought. If he hadn't been so obnoxious through drink I could almost have liked him.

She was shaking with rage at the audacity of the man she had just left, but at the same time feeling pleased with the way she had dealt with the situation. All the way back to Church House she alternated between being somewhat excited and bewildered by his advances, no matter how inappropriate, and mystified as to why Clive was so hostile towards Tim.

She arrived back at the house and tried to calm herself down. She made a cup of tea in the kitchen, although if it had been later in the day a glass of wine would have been better, then went through to the sitting room. Still slightly shaking she went over to Tim's CD collection. She hadn't looked at it in detail before but looking through now she saw that he had an eclectic taste in music. There were all kinds of genres and most of them she liked. He had loads of stuff from the early 80's, Bruce Springsteen, David Bowie and Prince were CDs that caught her attention along with some other questionable choices such as The Communards and The Pet Shop Boys. She wouldn't have thought they were his sort of thing.

She took a few of the CDs from the shelf to have a closer look. He also had a pretty good selection of jazz and classical music too. We have more in common than I thought, she pondered. She picked out Bach's Toccata and Fugue in D Minor as her choice at that particular time. The moment she put the CD on, the beautiful organ sound that she had always loved since childhood engulfed her and she felt its calming tones starting to soothe her edgy nerves.

She settled down on the sofa and tried to collect her thoughts. She was going to tell Tim about her incident with Clive. She wanted to know why he had spoken with such contempt about Tim? He had mentioned something about his son being at Tim's school but she couldn't understand what could have happened to make him hate Tim so much. He also seemed to be suggesting doubts over the nature of Sam's death and possibly questioning Tim's sexuality. She had no doubts on that sphere with what she had experienced in bed with him so far.

***

When Tim arrived back at the house in the early afternoon, the day had obviously taken its toll on him. Posy heard him come in, slam the door hard and start to climb the stairs. She thought that he had forgotten she was there and called out. She went to turn down the music and as she was doing so he walked in to the sitting room.

At first she was surprised at his greeting. He looked exhausted and appeared rather tetchy, but then his mood changed and he seemed pleased to see her. He came over and flung his arms around her giving her a big hug.

He said he'd been training with the local rugby team who were mostly young lads but there were a few older players and he'd enjoyed it. It brought back memories of when he played for his school and, at one point, he thought that he could take up the sport professionally. He would go to all the local team's matches to spur them on and sometimes, if he wasn't busy with other things, he would train them when their usual coach was away. He was tired as after he'd finished with the training he'd then had to go to the hospital in Oxford to visit a dying parishioner and console her family.

He perceptively sensed by her countenance that there was something wrong. Posy told him the whole story of how she had met Miranda Cameron-Clarke in the pub the previous day and that she had been invited for coffee today only for Miranda to not be there. Her husband had been there however, and appeared to be drunk and had made a lecherous pass at her.

Tim's face went white and he looked

serious. Posy thought that she could see a tremor in his hand and he bit his lip. He explained why Clive Cameron-Clarke had a reason to hate him and what had happened all those years ago when he had been the headmaster of a prestigious boys school and Clive's son had been one of his pupils. In his view, his son was a nasty, privileged, spoiled brat.

He'd been in trouble plenty of times mainly for bullying. However, the final straw came when the boy, Rupert, had coerced an underage girl into having sex with him, which he'd recorded on his mobile phone. To make it worse he had then proceeded to distribute the film around the school. He'd been found out by one of the prefects who'd had issues with Rupert before and he was disgusted by his latest antics and reported it to the Headmaster. Rupert was duly brought to task and Tim had no other option than to expel him. The Cameron-Clarke's had been furious, said it was a set-up and that they would tarnish Tim Woburn Smith's name so that he would never work again. They knew people in high places and could make life difficult, very difficult for him. Tim knew that he'd made an enemy but also knew that he had made the right and only proper decision in expelling Rupert Cameron-Clarke.

Tim had moved to Bolingbroke and was happily settled in and starting a new life, when the Cameron-Clarkes had bought the Manor House and were virtually his neighbours. He couldn't believe the coincidence and his bad luck at having them so close but he knew that virtue and God were on his side.

Tim looked at Posy, 'I think that this is a very nasty situation and by the sounds of it might even have been set up. I can't leave this. I'm going to sort it out and I'm going round there now.' His voice was shaking.

He went to go out of the door and get into his car but Posy stopped him. She tried to calm him down and persuaded him to leave it for a while.

'Best to sleep on it, he's just a very unpleasant man with an obvious drink problem. I thumped him anyhow so I got the better of him in the end.'

The following morning Tim had gone off to work and Posy was just pottering around upstairs. It was Mrs Chiltern's day to come and clean the house. Posy thought she heard the sound of horse hooves outside and then the doorbell ringing. After a while there was a knock on the bedroom door and Mrs Chiltern stood outside.

'It's Mrs Cameron-Clarke from the Manor for you. She's come on her horse. Left it tied up to the gatepost. Hope it doesn't make a mess on the pathway. Anyway I've shown her into the sitting room.' She sniffed with a slight air of disapproval.

Posy thanked Mrs Chiltern. What on earth could Miranda want, was she coming round to apologise for not being at home yesterday? Did she know what had happened between Posy and her husband? She looked out of the window and sure enough there was a large chestnut horse tethered up to the stone gatepost. Posy didn't have much equine knowledge, not being a rider, but it certainly looked like a well-bred specimen. Quite majestic and tall with it's glossy coat scrupulously groomed and gleaming.

She tentatively went downstairs and entered the sitting room. Miranda was standing there in her riding boots looking objectively at the books on the shelf.

'Oh Posy, I've come round to apologise for yesterday. I hope you didn't go to the house. I completely forgot until I saw Vicky this morning and she asked how it had gone when you came round. I thought, Oh goodness, I feel so awful. If you did go I'm surprised Clive didn't tell me as he was home yesterday. But, then again I know he wasn't feeling well. He had a fall, apparently in the bathroom and hit his head on the basin, he's got a terrible bruise.'

Posy gave a small inward smile and had to forgive her, poor woman. Clive obviously hadn't said anything about their little debacle and she was unaware of his advances towards her. She offered her a coffee and they went into the kitchen together to make it.

As they were waiting for the kettle to boil Miranda, who was not the sort of person to hold back on things, asked Posy how long she had actually known her vicar fiancé for. Posy wasn't going to go into detail and tell her about her son dying and his heart being donated to Tim's son, that was too personal. She just said, 'Oh, since last summer,' which was true.

Posy made the coffee and offered Miranda a biscuit which she declined, waving the tin away as if it would poison her to eat one.

'It's just that we've known Tim for a number of years, since our son was at the school where he was headmaster.'

Posy feigned ignorance of this fact. 'Oh really.'

'Yes, there was a bit of trouble with Rupert. To be absolutely honest Rupert was rather a little shit and deserved to be expelled for what he did. He's turned his life around since then though and is doing really well in the City. It's just on another matter, we have a great friend, Alan, he has a large, very successful, building company and he, um, sort of, knew Samantha, Tim's wife, rather well.'

Posy was now starting to get interested in the conversation.

'Oh really, did Tim know him as well?'

'No, I mean, Sam and Alan were having an affair. I think they were rather serious about each other and she was going to divorce Tim. Not sure about it but that's what I gathered. Anyway, there was an awful scene apparently when Tim found out and then she died that day. I don't want to be a tittle tattle but Alan said she had been absolutely fine up to that point so it all seemed rather strange. She apparently had a terrible time with Woburn Smith and his issues. He made a big thing of being bereft when she died.'

Miranda took another sip of her coffee and

looked at Posy eager for her reaction.

'Gosh, I've completely forgotten about Myrtle, my horse, I tethered her up outside. I'd better be going. Listen, give me a call anytime you want a chat. I sincerely mean it and I'm totally sorry about yesterday. It's just with three horses and trying to run a business as well it's rather frantic.' She pulled a card from her jacket pocket and handed it to Posy. The card showed her as Miranda Cameron-Clarke, Interior Designer and gave her contact details..

'Okay, yes, I'd be interested to chat more,' said Posy as she led her out through the front door. Miranda went to collect her horse, untied her, mounted and waved goodbye to Posy and with a kick of her heels rode off.

Posy went back inside the house, reeling from what she had just heard and feeling rather confused and slightly wary about things with Tim. She would make her own decisions. She knew the way she felt about him and so far the Cameron-Clarkes hadn't impressed her much.

***

It wasn't long after Miranda had left when

Posy's mobile phone rang. Looking at the screen she didn't recognise the number.

'Hello,' she answered.

She was surprised when she heard Clive Cameron-Clarke's voice on the other end.

'I owe you an apology for yesterday, dear lady,' he said. 'I was drunk. There had been a terrible row with my wife that morning. She had stormed out threatening to divorce me and take every penny I had. You turned up at the door. The connection between Woburn Smith and yourself just brought back all the troubles I'd had with my son at that time and I behaved in a most inappropriate fashion. There is no excuse for it; I have only myself to blame. I sincerely hope you will accept my apology. I certainly commend you on your Taekwondo punch though. That was quite a belter you gave me. I've got quite a bruise that I had to explain away.'

Posy was amazed at his apology and had to admit that she could imagine life would be pretty hard going living with Miranda judging by the short period she had known her.

She agreed that she would forgive him which he was relieved about.

'Could we meet up as I would very much like to talk further with you.'

'No I don't think so,' she replied 'but I don't hold any grudges towards you. Don't worry.'

She hung up the phone feeling slightly bemused by all these goings on.

***

That box of love letters to Sam from Alan, they were still in the cupboard in the bedroom. What more secrets were waiting to be uncovered? She was intrigued by the solicitor's letter, but she made the decision to dispose of the whole lot of them. Sam was dead anyway. It would serve no purpose to upset Tim to know about them. Haydn now knew as he had overheard her talking with Chloe but she wasn't sure about Tim and they would be best disposed of.

Posy went upstairs and checked that there was only one box that contained private written material and she was relieved to find that the other boxes contained just shoes. She managed to smuggle the shoe box out of the house and in to her car where she would take it back to her home and burn the contents. She was determined that curiosity would not get the better of her and prompt her to have a look at the content of the letters once she was in the privacy of her own house. This was someone's personal life and not for her eyes. Her training and years as a nurse had taught her great respect for other people's, not only possessions, but emotions, and that included their private letters. Besides which, she felt it better that she didn't know what had gone on between Tim's wife and her lover. That was much too intrusive. Now she had agreed to marry Tim and become his second wife she wanted to start their life together with a clean slate.

Was there any truth in what Clive and Miranda had been implying about Sam's death? She sincerely hoped not. They were bitter towards him because they thought he had treated their son unfairly, at least that's how she viewed it.

Posy left Church House the next morning and on her return home the first thing she did was burn the shoe box in her garden. She lit some newspaper and put it on the box. It was as dry as tinder and went up in flames immediately. She watched the red and yellow flames turn to blue and then the smoke as the letters of love and any other clues to the state of her lover's marriage were lost forever into the ashes.

'I'm sorry Sam, maybe you were a lovely person and I'm sorry about what happened to you but the past is the past and it's time to move forward now.' She felt sure that she had done the right thing and went back into her house with a completely clear conscience. She only wished that she didn't have this little niggling doubt that Miranda and Clive had placed in her mind. She knew they had an axe to grind about their son and his contretemps with his headmaster but Samantha's sudden death was another thing.

CHAPTER SIXTEEN

They married quietly at the registry office
in Oxford one Wednesday morning in August.
It was just a year since they had first met and
things had surely moved fast but, neither
wanted to waste any time. There was that
Carpe Diem again!

Tim had had his fill of weddings and just
couldn't face all the rigmarole first of
choosing who was to marry them and then
making all the preparations. By going to the
registry office, he hadn't offended any of his
ecclesiastical colleagues and the Registrar did
an excellent job anyway. He was still booked
up most Saturdays with weddings and wanted
to sneak off quietly for his own. Mr Harvey
was continuing with his back-breaking job of
sweeping up confetti at most of these but
enjoyed this duty immensely and was there at
the Registry Office to wish them both luck.

It was only their closest relatives in
attendance with Angharad as a witness with

Jeff in tow and Nancy Wagstaffe had come along as well to represent the Parish. They had a meal prepared waiting for when they returned to Church House and it was all organised by Posy in her own down-to-earth, unflappable manner. Word had gone around the village and there was a splendid display of flowers and all sorts of presents and delicious dishes had been delivered by well-wishing parishioners to the house. Tim and Posy were stunned by the congregation's generosity. It was obvious that Tim was a much-loved incumbent.

Posy had poached a whole salmon and beautifully decorated it with cucumber and lemon slices to look like scales. She had done this the night before, a welcome distraction from the nerves of getting married the next day. There was a wonderful buffet for the guests consisting of potato salad, coleslaw, four different kinds of quiche, a wonderful salad that must have been Middle Eastern in origin and contained aubergine, pomegranate and the most delicious spicy yoghurt dressing possible. A completely home-grown, all-organic salad graced the table compliments of Chloe Woburn Smith. Puddings consisted of a traditional (lots of sherry) trifle lovingly created by Nancy Wagstaffe, and a very elegant chocolate mousse laced with lashings of brandy and decorated with chocolate-dipped strawberries that Susan Woburn Smith had brought. All this was complemented with Champagne and well cooled Sauvignon Blanc.

Mark, Tim's rugby friend was best man and he said a few words and gave a toast to the bride and groom. Posy had noticed Susan talking to him animatedly earlier and she seemed to know him fairly well, so she felt slightly concerned that she hadn't been introduced before. She had asked Tim if they could invite him for dinner a few times so she could get to know him but there had always been something else going on. On her first impression she thought he seemed a decent enough guy and was very charming towards her. He was good looking in a rugged way and she was surprised that he had never been married or wanted to bring a girlfriend with him to their wedding.

Mark's speech was followed by a few words from Haydn which brought Posy to tears when he mentioned how his father and Posy had met and referred with grateful thanks and love to Josh.

Nancy Wagstaffe stood up to congratulate the happy couple and wish them the best of luck in their future partnership. She was heaping praise on Tim's ability as a parish priest and all that he had done for the village. She lightened the mood by telling an amusing story of how he apparently had a hotline to God and the story of what had happened at a Parish Church Council meeting one evening in the church hall.

'We were all sitting around the big glass table in there and above was a light fitting with a very expensive Tiffany glass and leaded shade which had been a gift from one of the parishioners, George Parkin it was, lovely man. Anyway, he had left it to the church in his will. There was an unholy row going on between the members of the Parochial Church Council and a representative couple of parishioners who were affronted because a hedge in the churchyard had been cut down while birds were nesting there. They had heard that there were also plans to cut down a very old yew tree and they felt it was damage of a criminal nature. It had been reported to the planning authorities but by then it was too late for the hedge and the birds. The whole village had been in uproar over this. Mr Harvey, as Churchwarden, was trying to placate them by explaining that it had been done as a Health and Safety issue but this caused even more disruption and trouble.'

Nancy gave a little nod over to Mr Harvey who was sitting in the corner sipping on a glass of wine.

'Then just as the main protestor, who here shall remain nameless - ahem, but we all know who *she* is,' she said putting her finger to her lips, getting her timing right and looking for a reaction. The *she* in question was a meddlesome woman in the village who had been on the Parish Council Committee but had caused so many problems and angst within the village that she had politely been asked to resign from the Committee much to her chagrin.

'*She* was just about to launch into another angry shouting match when Tim shouted 'silence'. At that moment, there was an almighty crash as the lamp shade came crashing down onto the glass table and subsequently smashed into thousands of pieces causing screams of shock. It was like a bolt from heaven. Everyone just stopped still and stared in awe at what had happened. It certainly shut them all up. Hence, thereafter we all joked that Tim had "a hotline to God." and now he's been sent his angel.

So now, I propose a toast and all the best for a long and happy marriage to Tim and Posy.'

And with that, amidst much amusement from the wedding party, she took a large swig of Champagne and sat down.

Posy looked at Tim and something unnerved her for a split second, and she hoped that she had made the right decision in marrying him. Too late to have last minute doubts now, she had done the deed. Maybe it had all happened too quickly, whilst she was still grieving, but then she knew he was a good man and it brought her closer to Haydn and through him to Josh.

***

'We'll have to go somewhere hot and romantic for our honeymoon,' Tim had said. 'What about one of the Greek islands, or even let's splash out and try somewhere in the Caribbean? I've never been there and would like to see what all the fuss is about. Apparently the beaches are amazing.'

He couldn't believe it when Posy told him that she had never been on an aeroplane in her life and didn't particularly want to either. She didn't like the idea of using all that fossil fuel and couldn't see the point in going further afield as there were so many places she still wanted to see in the UK. In the end they came to a compromise. They would go to Jersey for their honeymoon and take the car on the ferry. Then, just as they were about to book it; Posy changed her mind about flying. She felt that she shouldn't be such a wimp and she should try flying so the decision was made and they would go by plane.

Once they'd made their decision they pored over which hotel to book and finally chose a lovely looking hotel right on the beach at St Brelade.

As their honeymoon week grew closer, Posy's excitement was increasing at having her first holiday off the shores of the UK.

'Not many people of your age have never been on a plane before,' laughed Tim. She didn't care what people thought and so what if it was unusual that she hadn't flown before. She'd been to plenty of beautiful places all over her own country and thought that was more of an achievement these days. As it was her first experience of flying, she felt a few butterflies but she had to admit it wasn't as bad as she had imagined. The worst part of the experience in her view was the hanging around and security checks at the airport.

Once they'd settled on the plane, with her hand firmly placed in Tim's she looked down to admire her lovely emerald and diamond engagement ring and the new, gold wedding band. The rush of the engines as they ascended into the sky was a challenge for her and she felt her heart beating faster at the excitement. As the plane took off and soared upwards, she looked down upon the mass of soft cotton like clouds that floated below. Now and then, there was a break in the clouds which allowed a glimpse of the land below that shortly turned into sea. The sea was a beautiful turquoise green colour; the ripples on its surface looked like small bumps and here and there she could spot boats which looked like tadpoles with white froth tails moving slowly in the shimmering blue green water.

As they approached the Island she could see a long stretch of golden beach and houses, many with swimming pools, the oblong patches of blue a contrast between the green fields and small dots that appeared to be cows.

They spent a good deal of their honeymoon discovering the Island, having long cliff top walks in the sunshine and dipping their toes into the water as they walked along the beach. They visited Gorey and climbed the several hundred steps to the top of the castle there. Looking out from the top over to the coast of France, the nearest point being only 14 miles away, Posy felt as though you could almost swim it. France looked like a hop away with just the sparkling sea in between. Locals were enjoying their boats and she watched as a small fishing boat came into the harbour. As they moored up she saw the fishermen offloading their catch of the day and putting it in the waiting van ready to be delivered straight to the fish market in St Helier.

They made the most of being by the seaside and went in the sea a couple of times, flinching as they first went in, the water still feeling cold despite it being August, it was the Atlantic after all. As they became acclimatised to the water they started enjoying it and vowed to visit the seaside more when they had returned home. Gloucestershire was a fair drive to the coast though, and they knew they most likely wouldn't live up to their promise. They enjoyed the freshly caught lobster, crab and moules mariniere that were on offer in one of the restaurants that they had discovered and found to be their favourite. They returned there a number of times and were impressed when the restaurant manager recognised them and greeted them welcomingly on each subsequent visit.

'You know I love being here so much. My dream would be to have a house by the sea. Would it be possible that we could move to Jersey?'

Tim laughed, 'Lovely idea but it's almost impossible to move to Jersey and buy a house unless you have millions of pounds. I'd love to be able to do that for you Posy but on a vicar's wage it's out of my reach I'm afraid. Still, who knows? Someday we may be able to live by the sea.'

'Oh, I'd love that,' Posy replied hopefully.

They decided to visit Sark on a boat trip one day. 'I've heard there is no traffic there at all, only tractors and a few horses,' said Posy. This appealed to her very much so they asked the hotel receptionist to book it for them.

'It has been quite choppy on the sea the last few days,' warned the receptionist.

They arrived at the harbour early in the morning eager and looking forward to their first visit to Sark. The wind had certainly got up outside, but the sea looked smooth enough in the harbour. There seemed to be a few slight, white horses in the distance but it was only a short trip, just over an hour they had been told.

As they waited in the ferry terminal several of their fellow passengers seemed to be unsure whether the ferry was going or not.

'I've heard it's touch and go whether it's going to sail,' she overheard one anxious passenger querying. There seemed to be a discussion going on about the weather and the sailing.

'Is it often cancelled then?' asked Posy fearfully to one of the other tourists waiting to board.

'No, I don't think so, but a Force 8 has been forecast and it's getting pretty choppy out there. It's only a small ferry and not sure it can take that sort of sea,' answered an elderly man who was holding his wife's hand and looking rather apprehensive.

Posy started to have misgivings about their day trip. It sounded rather ominous to her and she didn't like the sound of a Force 8 either.

She had been on a few boats in her time but never encountered bad seas on them. She looked out of the terminal window. It seemed like a pleasant day and the sun was shining.

'Are you a good sailor, Tim?' she tentatively asked her new, now slightly worried looking husband who had been holding her hand plus the bag they had brought of emergency supplies, such as water, plastic glasses, packets of crisps and, not least, a bottle of wine.

'I've been on a few boats and ferries in the past and been sailing with the kids at school a few times. I used to row a bit when I was at school too. So I think I am a fairly good sailor, yes.'

The steward called them to board and they filed out of the terminus onto the quay, then boarded the gangway and embarked the boat. It was a small ferry but looked fairly new and spotlessly clean, which Posy and Tim were relieved to see. They noticed the paper bags placed in front of every seat and looked at each other. Making light of these, Tim said, 'I wonder what those are for?' Posy raised her eyes upwards and crossed herself mockingly.

They chose seats in the central part of the boat and settled down for what they thought would be a comfortable ride and a lovely day ahead of them discovering the beautiful Island of Sark.

The journey started well and Posy was feeling happy and relaxed as the ferry slowly made its way out of the harbour gates. They were both looking forward to their romantic day out and exploring the island that they had been told was like stepping back in time. Possibly they might find an isolated, quiet field and make love there. They had tried doing that in the countryside around Bolingbroke but Tim had been too worried about one of his parishioners coming upon them and somehow this had dampened his ardour. Today, however, they wouldn't know anybody. It would be exciting. Little bit of wine, sunshine, beautiful scenery lots of love: what could be better?

Suddenly the boat started to lurch to the side. Then it lurched to the other side. They had only just left the harbour and it seemed quite choppy. For a few minutes it quietened down. Posy breathed a premature sigh of relief, since the boat then rose at the bow and came crashing down again. They could see giant waves ahead of them. Several of the passengers screamed.

'Oh dear,' said Tim reaching for the paper bag which somehow seemed quite relevant now. Posy noticed that he had gone very pale with a slight green tinge around his jawline. She grabbed his hand just as the boat crashed back down onto the water again. She couldn't ever remember feeling so scared and only another 40 minutes to go. This was meant to be an enjoyable day out but it was turning into a nightmare. In the end she just buried her head in Tim's lap and hoped she could train her thoughts to think of something else. Poor Tim however was being violently sick along with many of the other passengers.

The nightmare journey eventually came to an end as they approached Sark. The sea seemed to calm down and it became more comfortable.

'I am not setting foot on this ferry again until it is less stormy. If this means we have to stay the night here, fine, I'll pay for it!' bemoaned Posy to a now slightly more colourful looking Tim.

'Yes, as soon as we get there we'll check with the harbourmaster what the weather is forecast for the trip back and if it's still going to be rough we'll find somewhere to stay.'

They disembarked with the other fairly

shaken up passengers and immediately headed up to see the Harbourmaster at the end of the pier sitting in his wooden cabin. They asked him what the forecast was like and if they could get the ferry back tomorrow instead.

'Well, there isn't a ferry tomorrow I'm afraid. They only go every other day. On the way back though the tide will be going out so it will be a much smoother ride. The trick is to sit right at the very back of the ferry and you don't feel the bumps so much there.'

Oh God thought Posy. We can't stay here for two nights, we're going home the day after tomorrow and we'd miss our plane. We'll just have to chance it.

They did find a field but making love in the wild again was not to be. Feeling relaxed after the terrible boat trip the day was redeemed by the glorious scenery that they encountered and a few sips of wine from the bottle they had brought with them. Settling down on Tim's jacket that he'd placed on a tufty piece of grass Posy felt confident in her new marriage and somehow, it seemed the right time to bring up the subject of Sam. They had never spoken about her and it had been niggling her. She had to have this conversation.

'Tim, were you honestly happy in your marriage to Sam?'

Tim told Posy how he knew his marriage had hit a rocky patch and probably hadn't been all it should have for a number of years.

'I suppose I was partly to blame. I was so immersed in my work.' He remembered how he would often be away for weeks on end training at theological college and when he wasn't doing that he was organising rugby matches for the local team or involved with the charity that he was a patron of.

'Then when I was at home, I guess I was spending time with Haydn in compensation for being away so much. I think Sam was incredibly lonely.' He hesitated and clenched his jaw as he looked out pensively over the fields to the sea beyond.

There was a silence between them, but Posy had been brave enough to broach the subject to this point and couldn't leave the matter unfinished.

'So what did you do; did you talk to her about it or go to marriage counselling?' urged Posy.

'No, I didn't, much to my sorrow. Unknown to me she met this chap at the school where she worked. I'd left there by this stage to train for priesthood. He was a builder, the father of one of the pupils. I think that she asked him to do some work at our house and it all started like that and then progressed, and they started an affair. I had absolutely no idea at the time but apparently it had been going on for a couple of years before I found out.'

'I would go off to London to the college where I was studying and he would come and visit Sam. Haydn was away at his boarding school and then he went to agricultural college so she had plenty of time alone and our house was fairly remote so no peeping neighbours. It was an ideal situation for her to have an affair and I had no idea. It was horrible, the worst day of my life when I found out. I had left college early to come home. I saw a car in the drive that I didn't recognise, but thought it was probably a friend of Sam's come round for a chat. I walked into the house and there was no sign of her so I shouted out and went upstairs. When I walked into the bedroom there they were with him frantically trying to get dressed. She had her hair all over the place and her make up was all smudged, it was so obvious what they had been up to. I was incensed. He made himself scarce and left me to try and pick up the pieces. Sam just wasn't having it though, she was shouting at me. She said some really hurtful things about how she didn't love me, had never loved me. She said I was a useless lover and she wanted to be with this Alan character. He loved her and she wanted to leave me.'

'Well, I just lost it. I snapped, I really saw red and I know the meaning of that now and how true a saying it is. I struck out, I had never felt anger like it, please believe me I have never done this before and I would never, ever do it again but I shook her. It was only a shake, not a punch or a hit but just a shake. I'll never forget the way she looked at me with a look of complete shock on her face and fell to the floor and started hyperventilating. At first I thought she was just play acting to scare me but then I realised it was for real. She was gasping and saying she couldn't breathe and had pains in her chest.'

Tim remembered how he'd tried to help her with First Aid but when he realised it was serious he had dialled the emergency number for an ambulance. Tim broke down at this stage as he remembered that terrible day and he sobbed in Posy's arms.

'She died in the ambulance on the way to the hospital. Her heart just gave out. I felt so guilty, I felt as though I had murdered her. It was terrible, I don't think I've ever had problems with anger before, but this situation just took me completely by surprise and I can't believe how I reacted. I had to break the news of her death to Haydn and he took it seemingly calmly and well. I guess he had been prepared for something like this as he had known about his mother's health problems.'

'There was a post mortem as it was a sudden death and she had some unexplained bruising. The results showed that she had died from long term heart disease so there didn't need to be an inquest. However, there were plenty of malicious rumours going around which was very hurtful.'

Posy looked at him with an earnest expression in her eyes. She knew about deceit and the dangerous feelings it could stir. Tim, who appeared such a caring, gentle person being spurred into violence showed how deeply he had felt about the situation. She totally believed that what he did was entirely out of character but was caused by the passion he had felt at his wife's betrayal.

'The bastard even had the audacity and gall to come to her funeral. He bought the most ostentatious flower display possible. I knew who he was but couldn't bear to look at him, he just made me feel sick. I couldn't live at the house after that. I was lucky enough to get the job in Bolingbroke with the house that came with it. Haydn and I moved pretty quickly then and rented the old house out. I can never go back there, there are too many memories.'

Posy was no stranger to painful memories. 'I know what you mean. I found it very difficult being in my house after Josh died but it's only bricks and mortar. People are the important things in life not houses or possessions. In fact, when we get back I should put my house on the market. We don't need another house now we're married.'

'Yes, I agree with you. I'm getting a good rental for my old house at the moment but maybe if you sell your house and I sell mine then I could slow down with work a bit and we could move somewhere by the sea,' suggested Tim looking out over the field to the cliffs beyond. The sea was twinkling below, plenty of white horses still visible from their rough crossing.

'Posy, please believe me, I've never told anyone else about this before about Sam's final hours, I trust you, you're my wife now.'

Posy was surprised at how readily he opened up to her, seemingly as though it was a confession. He had confided in her, she was privy to his secret and it was as if he was asking for forgiveness.

She was astounded by his outburst but she saw how sincere he was and felt privileged that he could share his innermost feelings to her. She had a few more questions that she needed answering though, when the time was right. He had lost his temper towards Sam but then she had been having an affair and he'd just found out, what man in his right mind wouldn't be angry.

CHAPTER SEVENTEEN

The newly-weds settled down into their life together at Church House, Tim, still as busy as ever with matters regarding the Parish and Posy starting at her new job as practice nurse.

The secret they shared regarding Sam's final hours was to remain just theirs, and with this knowledge she felt they had a special if slightly unnerving bond.

She'd been out with Angharad for the day and as they were walking through Oxford she started noticing feathers. She pointed them out to Angharad.

'That's surely a sign. I read somewhere that feathers can be seen as fallen from an angel. A reminder of a special person's love; a guardian angel watching and protecting from above.'

She seemed to see them floating down from the sky as if a little bird had decided to shed them especially for her. Everywhere she walked she would see little feathers on the ground and stoop to pick them up. Sometimes, she would notice them fluttering down from the sky and try to catch them before they landed on the ground. She would look up to see if she could spot the host who had discarded it, but the bird had usually flown away soaring up and away from her in the warm current of air. She wondered had there always been so many feathers around or did she just have a heightened state of awareness? She wasn't sure, but to her it seemed as if they were messages from some supreme being, or maybe Josh; small offerings from angels, gifts from their wings. She had an idea that she had been toying with for a while. A tattoo, I know, I will get a tattoo.

When she was a child she was told by her father that tattoos were something merchant seaman had or labourers on building sites, not something that nice people had. Her father used to joke that if she was a naughty girl he would get a tattoo. 'Oh no daddy, please don't, I'll be good I promise,' she would cry. These days however, things were totally different and the body adornment was so popular that almost everybody she noticed had a tattoo somewhere. In fact it seemed almost unusual for a person not to have one. 'What I would like is just something very small and personal to myself. Something in memory of Josh that also symbolises new life and new love,' she thought.

After a bit of Google research Posy headed off into Oxford to check out some of the tattoo parlours there that had good reviews. She felt slightly ill at ease entering these places, out of her comfort zone, but once she had made the decision to go in they couldn't have been more pleasant and charming and the place looked scrupulously clean. She knew that she wasn't doing this on a whim, that wasn't in Posy's character. She knew what she wanted and she felt much more confident once she had met the tattoo artist, whose name was Jason. He was probably in his early forties, patently very experienced and with tremendous artistic flair judging from pictures of his previous work. She explained her reason for wanting a tattoo and he was very compassionate and understanding.

'I would just like a small heart with a feather either side on my left arm so when I put my arm down it's next to my heart. I don't wear short sleeves because I'm getting older and rather conscious of my upper arms so I want this very discreetly placed.' Jason spent nearly an hour with her going through images of what she might like. He suggested angel wings on either side of the heart would look appealing and he could make the heart red for extra effect. Posy said she would have to think about that idea, but it sounded like a pretty image and a lovely thought. He also explained to her about the actual tattooing procedure and the aftercare, which helped to reassure her.

'You don't have to make an immediate decision now. Have a think about it overnight,' he said genially, 'I'll book you in for tomorrow afternoon but if you have any doubts or hesitation just let me know, I quite understand that this is a very brave thing for you to do.'

Posy didn't have any hesitation though and the next day she turned up at the tattoo parlour in Oxford. Yes, the procedure did hurt a bit but she had her headphones on and some calming music which took her mind off things. When it was all done she looked at the finished article. A beautiful little heart with angel wings either side. She exclaimed, 'I love it!'

'It looks a bit raw at the moment,' said Jason 'but this is normal and will die down within two to three weeks. It could even take up to six months for it to truly heal but stick with the instructions I've given you and it will settle down and start to look good. I have to say that I'm very pleased with this one. I think it's a lovely tribute to your son.'

'It's perfect, thank you.' She paid him and he collected her coat and helped her on with it. Her arm did feel a bit sore as she lifted it up to put her arm in the coat sleeve, but she knew it wasn't anything to worry about. Being a nurse she would keep a close eye on it and keep it clean to prevent any infection whilst it was healing. She walked out of the tattoo shop. It was pouring with rain so she ran all the way back to the car park. She was soaked through but didn't care. She'd turn on the heater and would dry out quickly. Once in the car she sat there for a couple of minutes, collecting her thoughts and then after a while she started the car and drove home feeling elated and slightly surprised with herself at what she had done.

'Oh my God, I've done it,' she said out loud, 'Josh, I've got a tattoo and there was me telling you don't you ever get a tattoo and now your mother's gone and done it!'

It rained heavily all the way back to Bolingbroke and it was necessary to put the windscreen wipers on their fastest setting to clear the screen. When she arrived back at Church House she quickly ran in and went upstairs to get out of her damp clothes. As she carefully peeled off her jumper she took a look at her new tattoo, through the protective film. It looked very red and raw, but she had expected that and was looking forward to when it had all healed, and even though it wouldn't be on show much she was happy knowing that her little tribute was on her arm permanently.

She now suddenly felt exhausted after her trip to Oxford and the tattoo experience. She hadn't told Tim about getting a tattoo and she felt a little guilty about that. They had never had a discussion regarding body art and what his views were on tattoos, but she hoped he would love it as much as she did. She thought he would be receptive to it. After all, he was an open-minded man having been a headmaster and then a vicar. He'd had to have a broad outlook on life dealing with all kinds of people and situations, and she felt her little inking to be in very good taste.

She chose a loose shirt that she felt would be comfortable over her sore arm and carefully put it on. Shortly afterwards Tim entered the room and Posy felt a twinge of anxiety. Maybe she should have let Tim in on the secret that she was getting a tattoo. But why? It was her body and her decision. Anyway she wanted it to be a surprise.

It certainly was a surprise and didn't turn out quite the way she had been expecting.

'What have you been doing today, you've been gone a long time?' asked Tim.

'Yes, I went into Oxford. Actually I went and had a tattoo.'

'WHAT? You are joking aren't you, I hope you are.'

Oh dear, this wasn't quite the reaction that Posy was expecting. She could see tension flaring up in Tim's whole body language. She slowly rolled up the sleeve of her shirt and showed him the inking that was visible through the protective coating the tattoo artist had placed on it.

'I hate tattoos. How could you do this before discussing it with me? What prompted you to do this - is it a mid life crisis or something? You've scarred yourself for life. I didn't tell you that you could do this. The thing about tattoos is that they are permanent and they also put you in a category.' She saw a flash of anger in his eyes that she didn't like.

'Oh Tim. Please understand. It was something I wanted to do. Look it's a beating heart. It's in memory of Josh and also a tribute to Haydn, and there are angel's wings either side. Please don't be angry.'

Tim came towards her and grabbed hold of her wrist, twisting it as he brought her nearer to him. He had a furious look on his face and she started to feel intimidated. At that moment she felt threatened. This was not good; she felt scared of her own husband and his reaction to her decision because she had done something beyond his control.

'Tim, take your hands off me. This was my decision. I am an independent woman. Just because we are now married doesn't mean that I can't make my own choices. You know I had been on my own for a long time before I met you. If you are going to behave like this then I think we had better have another think about our relationship.'

Tim looked shocked at her outburst. He took his hands away from her and it was as though a switch had been turned off. He had a look of realisation. He quietly walked away from her and out of the room.

What have I done, have I married a monster? she asked herself. I know he has his moments of moodiness, but I really thought he was going to strike me then. He is a contradiction in terms; this man of God who is meant to be understanding and compassionate and yet someone who angers so quickly and doesn't understand the actions of another if it doesn't conform to his view. I wonder if this is what he was like with Sam; if so it could be one of the reasons why she was thinking of divorcing him.

She regretted her actions now in burning the letters in the shoe box. Maybe she would have found out some answers from reading them, especially the solicitor's letter, but it was too late now; they were gone. It was also too late for her; she had married him. Even though there was no doubt that she did feel love for him she was not sure if she loved him for the right reasons.

She went into the kitchen and made herself a cup of coffee, helped herself to a slice of cake from the tin of offerings that were always being dropped round by well-wishing parishioners and tried to calm herself down.

Once she'd finished her coffee she went upstairs to the bedroom she shared with Tim.

Tim didn't come to bed that night. Posy could see the light on in his study. He'd been in there for hours. She didn't know if she should go downstairs and try to placate him. To apologise for not consulting him on her tattoo decision. She decided against it. On one hand she was angry, disappointed at his reaction and rather afraid by his outburst. But, on the other hand, she could understand his upset at her not letting him in on her choice. Before I met Tim I had been on my own for a long time, she thought, I haven't had to answer to anybody for years and it's something I'm not used to.

She drifted off to sleep and was awoken by the door opening and a shaft of light from the corridor softly lighting the room.

'Posy, please wake up, I need to speak to you,' whispered Tim. He pulled back the cover slightly and placed his hand gently on her face.

'I'm so sorry for being angry with you. I've been thinking and I've made some decisions. I love you so much and I don't want to lose you. You deserve to be happy and I've been so inconsiderate and selfish. I realise now I had been focused on too many other things in my first marriage and I'd neglected the most important people to me; I don't want to repeat history. I'm finding the work I'm doing is causing me stress and that's why I get short tempered. It's no good, it can't go on and I've decided I'm going to resign from the ministry.'

Posy sleepily sat herself up in bed and looked at him. 'Oh Tim, you can't leave the Church, it's your love you would be lost without it.'

'No, it's not my love. It's a vocation but you are my love. I can't think of anything more important than you. I've been thinking long and hard about this all night. Do you think we should both put our houses on the market like we spoke about before and buy somewhere together, perhaps we can move to Devon? We could buy somewhere lovely by the sea which is what you said you've always wanted. We'll also be near Haydn and Chloe. What do you think? Perhaps I can do a little job down there so I'm not entirely retired, I don't think I could cope with complete retirement.' He looked at her pleadingly and she could see that he really meant it. She could sense that despite all his bravado he was actually vulnerable and he had been through a difficult time too. He had lost his wife and had to look after a sick son. He had had no one to look after him.

Posy felt a certain degree of concern for Tim. She knew deep down that he was a genuine and good person. She had a feeling that his anger issues were a by-product of his upbringing and his father's work ethic that had been drummed into him and to win at all costs. His decision to change his life around for her was a measure of his love for her.

'Tim, that sounds like the most fantastic idea. Yes, let's do it. But can we talk about it further in the morning I'm actually all done in now.'

He climbed into bed next to her and he held her for what was left of the night. She had a lot to think about. Was it because she could be nearer Haydn and therefore Josh that she had married him? There was his wife's sudden death, his mood swings, the accusations that the Cameron-Clarkes had put in her mind. There were doubts that she had to put to rest before she could be sincerely happy and know that she had done the right thing in marrying him. Were there any other secrets that were waiting to be uncovered?

CHAPTER EIGHTEEN

So that was settled then. Sell both houses and move to Devon. Posy couldn't wait. She contacted a local estate agent who she trusted. She knew that he would market her house well on his website and on social media. He knew all the right people and was way ahead of his competitors in the business. She trusted him implicitly which was a mental comfort for her as she was living a couple of hours away and the house was left unoccupied for most of that time.

Trevor knew her property from when it had first been built and advised that houses like hers were in high demand. He had no doubt that it would sell at the full asking price within a few months. It was within easy reach of London and yet still fairly rural and had a manageably sized garden, so was ideal for commuters. He was right; and within a few months it was all done and dusted. She sold much of the furniture and kept only the things that were of sentimental value to her or worth keeping.

She was sad at the thought of leaving the house permanently as it had so many memories of Josh, but he was always there with her, indelibly stamped in her mind and in her heart. His memory would follow her forever. He was also still alive in Haydn and as long as Haydn lived there would be that piece of him that was still beating. After all a house was only bricks and mortar, just another possession and she now also had a fairly healthy bank balance for the first time in her life

Tim was true to his word and handed in his notice to the bishop.

'*It is with great sadness that I have taken the decision to resign my licence and leave the Church of England,*' the resignation letter started and went on to explain his various reasons for leaving.

Posy thought the tone of the letter sounded rather pompous, but he assured her that things had to be formal and done in a certain way. She had to admit that she didn't know much about the ways of clergy protocol. This was his domain and much as she respected it she couldn't always accept the doctrine and guidelines that he had to comply with. All she could see was the man that he was and he seemed to be lighter in character because of his decision; as though a great weight had been lifted from him.

The next week he penned another letter, this one was to his parishioners, to be read out in Church at his succeeding service and to be sent out in the parish magazine:

Dear Parishioners

After much prayer and consideration it is my difficult duty to announce that I have given in my resignation as vicar of St Mary's, Bolingbroke. It is anticipated that my last Sunday will be in three months' time.

There are many reasons for reaching this decision but time is perhaps the most important. As you know I have recently married and my wife, Posy, works long hours during the week at the doctor's surgery, while my duties mean I work weekends and many evenings. On average we've ascertained that we will only be able to spend two full days a month together and as a newly-wed couple we feel that this isn't enough.

In addition, I personally find that I do not have enough time to 're-create' and charge my batteries, so to speak. I am aware that sooner, rather than later, I will start burning out and that will help no one. I would still like to keep up my charity work but in a lesser capacity, and I will have to resign from the rugby team training as we shall no longer be in the County. However, rather than give up the ministry altogether I anticipate moving back into a chaplaincy role which (God willing) will fit better with our family circumstances.

I am very aware that many of you have devoted much time and energy in supporting me and my son when he was living in the parish. Now that he is married and has moved away to start a new life, I myself am also on a new journey and would like to thank you all personally for your support. I hope that you will understand my decision and hope too that I have left a good foundation for the next vicar who will serve your parish. The bishop and archdeacon have assured me that they will do all they can to support the ongoing ministry and find the best replacement possible for me.

With many blessings and wishing peace to you all.

Reverend Tim Woburn Smith

Once the word spread around the village that the vicar was leaving, there were many phone calls and visitors to the house to say they were sorry the couple would be leaving. Tim was relieved and knew that he had made the right decision, but Posy was starting to enjoy her job at the surgery and much as the sea was calling her the countryside felt like home to her now.

***

It was getting to that time of year once more, the time when the lawn had started growing in abundance and bedding plants such as petunias, marigold and lobelia were in the garden centres ready to be planted out to be enjoyed throughout the summer. It was also the time when she started to hear the cuckoos calling to each other once more over the fields. The sound that she used to love now filled her with a sense of foreboding. She remembered listening to them calling the fateful night of Josh's accident, and now whenever she heard them it seemed like an omen, a bird of prophetic significance. She heard the cuckoo calling and was startled when the phone rang. She went tentatively into the sitting room to answer it. Tim was already on the case and was answering it as she entered the room. It was Haydn.

Far from the phone call being bad news, it was exactly the opposite; it was the phone call that told them that they were expecting a baby in early December. Joyous, happy news of a new life, of things to look forward to, of little hands, tiny feet and first steps to watch and moments to treasure. Going to school with a new, too large uniform that 'they'll grow into soon,' nativity plays, scribbled drawings proudly presented to put on the wall and school photos of well-scrubbed, smiling children. All these lovely things to look forward to and for Posy this was now within her reach.

***

So 16th December came and the strangely coincidental arrival of little Timothy Joshua, or TJ, as he was going to be known. As soon as he was born he was checked out by the paediatric team. He had heart monitors and tests and his little, beating heart seemed sturdy and healthy. 'Let's hope to God we've beaten this cycle,' said Tim.

'Yes, in more ways than one,' she answered meaning not only the familial heart problems, but also Tim's anger issues, and she gave him a deliberate and what she hoped was an authoritative look. She still had doubts about her marriage to him but otherwise her life was happy. The most important thing to her now was this little baby that had just been born and she felt a tremendous feeling of relief that things were going to be okay health-wise with the little boy and more than likely with any other children the young couple might have in the future.

CHAPTER NINETEEN

Packing up and moving on is always daunting. In fact, it's one of life's most traumatic events ranking up there with the death of a loved one, separation, divorce, starting a new job and financial problems. As Church House was attached to the church and Tim had given his notice, they had to leave and had three months in which to prepare. A new life, in a new place by the sea at Exmouth. That is what they had planned. Everything she dreamt and could have hoped for. They went down to stay with Haydn and Chloe whilst they were house-hunting, but nothing had taken their fancy and time was now starting to go very quickly before they had to leave the Parish.

It was beginning to be a dilemma. Posy had started to love the village of Bolingbroke. She was torn between going with Tim to live by the sea and nearer her little 'miracle' adored grandson who she almost felt was Josh reincarnated, and staying in Bolingbroke and the job that she was enjoying. She had made some good friends there. She'd go into the pub and chat with all the locals who had taken to her. She knew so many people due to her job at the surgery and most of whom she would miss.

She also had a new patient at the surgery. Highly confidential, of course, but Clive Cameron-Clarke had booked an appointment for a check up. His wife had left him. He knew that he had been drinking too much through stress, and being an intelligent man realised he needed help. Despite their previous disastrous meeting Posy was dealing with this like the professional she was. He actually was a very pleasant man she discovered. Like many successful people he had his demons but they weren't particularly bad ones. Posy admired him and no reference was made to their connection, but a friendship was growing, she could sense that, and there was an attraction there.

In the meantime, a dog joined the Woburn Smith household by circumstance. Tim had wanted a labrador which was 'a man's dog', as he had said, but Posy had befriended a lady in the village who needed to move into an apartment which wouldn't accept dogs. So that's how the little West Highland Terrier, Fifi, came into their lives.

'I think her little sticking up ears with the white silky fur look like angel wings,' said Posy.

'You've got a good imagination,' Tim retorted but he had grown very fond of the little dog too. They would walk her daily and go all round the village saying 'good morning' to people or whatever time of the day it was. Tim was relaxed knowing that his job was coming to an end and they were enjoying their life. But the time was getting nearer when they would have to move, and they were still no closer to finding anywhere. Posy started wondering if Tim's heart was really into this move and she noticed a distancing from him which worried her slightly.

He would still go off to rugby games with Mark. Posy would bundle Fifi into the car and go down to Devon and help out with Haydn and Chloe's gardening business or look after little TJ, so she was enjoying her life and didn't mind him going off to watch or play the sport that he enjoyed.

It was when he had been going away quite

often and she realised that it wasn't rugby season any longer that she started feeling things were not so normal. Tim's mood had started to change again and eventually she tackled him about it.

'Just what is wrong with you?' She said in desperation. 'Things were so brilliant for the first few months. You were much more relaxed once you'd given in your notice and I know you love going to see Haydn and TJ, but you're just not the same and you never kiss me any longer. We haven't been married for long and that's just not right.'

Tim looked at her and then turned his gaze away. He bit his lip and struggled to speak. Eventually it all just gushed out, exactly how he had been feeling and how troubled he was.

'I'm sorry but I have issues that I've been trying to deal with for years now and that I haven't been able to reveal. I've been praying that I can overcome my demons, but I realise now that it isn't possible to go on living a lie any longer.'

Posy looked at him aghast.

'What issues and what demons are you talking about?' She had an uneasy feeling; perhaps he had met another woman. She couldn't imagine Tim being a womaniser or cheating on her but she was worried what he could be referring to.

'I can't deny this any more. I've decided to be honest with you and myself, but I've been having struggles with the feelings I have for years now. When I was teaching at the boy's school I knew I would most likely, at that time, be dismissed if my secret came out. Then I had the calling to join the ministry, hoping that would help to stabilise my feelings. This only made it worse and I became increasingly dismayed at the Church's renewed hostility to the LGBT community and the rejecting of homosexual practice as incompatible to scripture. I know that things are changing rapidly, and thank God that they are, but it's still fraught with prejudice and stigma even in these days.

I realise that I haven't been fair on you and your happiness is so important to me especially after everything you have been through. I am so sorry that I haven't been honest with you before. I desperately tried and I do love you, but it's not enough.'

Posy gave him a hard look and tried to keep her voice in control

'Well, is there anyone special to you that you want to be with, rather than me?'

'Yes, there is someone special. It's Mark. I've always loved him but my feelings were so confused with everything I felt I should be. Even before I met Sam I knew how I felt about him but it was instilled in me that I had to conform. It wasn't right to love another man. I've struggled so much trying to do the right thing, but I just can't go on any longer living a lie. Mark has had the same problem throughout his life and we've both talked long and hard about this. We love each other and want to be together forever.'

With this confession Posy understood that you can never really get inside the mind of any other person. You can only guess at what is in somebody else's soul, just as they have only the faintest inkling of the depths and predilections of yours.

After a few seconds of thinking and remembering certain hints that might have predicted a clue of what the future held for their relationship she felt able to reply.

'Susan knew about this didn't she?'

'Yes, Susan has known about my sexual confusion since we were teenagers. She was urging me to tell you but I just couldn't do it. My mother will hopefully be accepting, but I do fear that my father, will be mortified. I've felt such a fraud all my life not knowing whether I wanted to be with a man or a woman and now I've involved you too, but none of it was out of malice. I genuinely do love you Posy but just not in the way that a man should love a woman. Please forgive me. I always want to be close to you, I just can't hide the way I feel about Mark anymore.'

She had been having doubts about her marriage to Tim over the last few months and it had dawned on her the realisation that she probably had never truly loved him. His news had become something of a relief, if she was being honest with herself. Had she wanted to be with him so that she was closer to Haydn and latterly baby TJ? It certainly made her feel closer to her darling Josh, as if he was still around with her.

Tim wasn't genuinely the sort of man that she could be with. She knew she was more of a free spirit than to be living with someone who wanted to control her.

'Well, if we're going to split up I want Fifi,' demanded Posy, albeit in a light hearted joking manner.

'Yes, you can keep her. As long as I have visiting rights,' smiled Tim.

Over the months that she had been getting to know him she knew that the man of her dreams was really Clive Cameron-Clarke. They were matches in character and she admired his dynamism and intellect. He was charismatic and charming, there was no doubt about that and she was falling in love with him.

Since Miranda had run off and left Clive for her wealthy horse trainer Posy knew he had been rather lost and struggling at the large house all on his own. He had been to see her in her capacity as the practice nurse at the doctor's surgery and she had been helping him with his drink problem. As Clive recovered from the break-up of his marriage, he was able to pull his life back together and end his reliance on alcohol for support.

EPILOGUE

The first time Tim met Posy White, who for a short time he proudly called his wife, Mrs Rosalind Woburn Smith, he had felt an instant connection. This was before he knew that her son had saved his son's life, and long before he knew how feisty and adorable she was.

He had wanted to please everyone in his life, his parents, especially his father who had always expected so much of him, his employers, the bishop, the parishioners and his sports colleagues. He figured that's why his life had revolved around work and helping others. Could he blame it on his upbringing or the way that men treated women at that time? No, he realised that he had to accept the issues which he had ultimately tried to deal with for all of his life. Struggling to come to terms with his gender fluidity and what it was that he really desired.

He felt guilty about his first wife, Samantha. Maybe if he'd given her more of his time and understanding she wouldn't have felt the need to seek love elsewhere, but she also knew his secret and she was going to let it out of the bag. He had never really desired her, that was the problem. For Posy however, he had truly felt sexually attracted to her and he hoped that he could come to terms with his errant feelings. She sometimes exasperated him by doing things that he totally couldn't comprehend, like getting a tattoo for example, but that was one of her endearing traits, her free spirit, her strong independence and her care for other people. He loved her but it was more as a friend and even though he'd tried to fight it he'd never really felt comfortable in a relationship with a woman.

He could no longer deny his inner passion for Mark and that it was true love and not just a platonic friendship. He was thankful that Posy understood and was surprisingly supportive of his dilemma. It certainly helped that she was now happily ensconced at Bolingbroke Manor with Cameron-Clarke. She had been his angel in seeing him through all this and for being so supportive. For the first time in his life he no longer needed to live a lie.

Tim resolved his differences with Clive. He even felt some compassion towards him, not for being with Posy, but because his wife had treated him very badly and then gone off with a champion horse trainer. Clive also admitted to Tim that his son had been totally in the wrong when he had been expelled, but the boy had turned his life around apparently and Tim felt in some way that this could have been thanks to his intervention.

The fact that Posy was putting the Manor and its grounds to good use and doing worthy works with transplant patients appeased Tim's conscience somewhat and he knew that she was happy and fulfilled. When she wasn't busy running her support groups she was having little TJ to stay and had plenty of opportunity to spend time with Haydn and Chloe as well. Baby number two was on the way too.

Clive, had turned out to be a thoroughly decent chap and when asked had helped Haydn and Chloe with their business both financially and with designs. They were on the way to fulfilling their dream of showing at Chelsea Flower Show. Their cutting-edge design proposal had been accepted and it was tipped for a gold medal.

The whole family were going up to London to see them exhibit at the great flower show. Tim and Mark were also meeting up with them all at a family get together in the evening.

***

With Tim happily settled with Mark and living in Exmouth, Posy moved into Bolingbroke Manor with Clive and quickly became accustomed to being chatelaine of the manor.

'Let's not get married, I rather like the idea of living in sin.' She had smiled at him. 'Besides which I don't think I could go through all that rigmarole again.'

Clive agreed whole-heartedly with her. He was pleased to have seen the back of Miranda and even though he'd had to pay her a large settlement it could have been much worse. She was living the high life among the horsy, racing set, and her new love was being generous to her which kept her off Clive's back.

Their relationship wasn't one of control on either side. They both listened and respected each other's views. When Posy suggested to Clive that she wanted to use the space at the manor for an idea that she had, he was very attentive.

'Come on then, spill the beans. What is this great idea you have?' Clive asked.

'Well, you know that I'm raising money for

charity but I haven't actually decided how to use it yet. Well, I've had an idea. With all this space we have and just the two of us here most of the time I would like to start up a centre for children who have undergone or are awaiting an organ transplant as well as their families. Do you think it's a good idea? They can come here to enjoy a holiday that they probably couldn't afford otherwise. They can make use of the gardens and we can run a support group. Through my contacts we can have medical experts come and give advice and talks and they can meet others in the same position as themselves.'

'I think that is an excellent idea, you are such an angel, my lovely Posy. You'll start growing wings soon like your tattoo,' said Clive admiringly. After being married to Miranda he couldn't believe his luck in finding such a paragon in Posy. He truly loved her and she had, at last, found the man she wanted to spend the rest of her life with.

'Just say the word and I'll help you financially or in any other way that I can.'

'Well, for a start, would you be able to design something that we could use as a Centre with bedrooms, games room and possibly a meeting room in the grounds?'

So that is how the Bolingbroke Organ Transplant Support Centre in loving memory of Josh White started.

She loved her architect, she loved the Manor House and most of all she loved her little grandson (and the two other little Woburn Smiths who followed in quick succession) who would not have come into being without her son's much-loved ever beating heart.

THE END

ACKNOWLEDGEMENTS

This is my first novel. It started as a short story and just grew from there. It has been inspired by many life events which have in reality happened to me, although some have been imagined. I'll leave it to the reader to decide which is real and which is imaginary.

I would like to thank all my family who have been so supportive and been there in the good times and the bad. I thank my wonderful husband, Nigel, who must have felt totally fed up when I said, yet again, from my laptop *'Does this sound right?'* or *'What's another word for…?'*

I thank my son-in-law, Jon, for encouraging me to write and for helping me with content and for editing, thanks also to Reverend Sandra Howells who gave me funny stories from life as a vicar. Also, thank you, to Richard Christensen for second editing and proof-reading.

Finally, I'd like to thank anyone I've ever met who has touched my life and left an indelible memory.

Hannah Leak, Jersey, Channel Islands, 2020

Printed in Great Britain
by Amazon